FIC.
KIL.   KILGORE, KATHLEEN
AUTHOR
           THE WOLFMAN OF BEACON HILL
TITLE

                                        NB1

DATE DUE	BORROWER'S NAME	ROOM NUMBER
MAR 21	Joshua McCully	41
APR 3	Tim Bergren	43
FEB 22	Sarah McCully	21
		13
DEC 28	Jamie B.	41
MAY 05	Tim Arche	

FIC.
KIL.   KILGORE, KATHLEEN   NB1

THE WOLFMAN OF BEACON HILL

WATERLOO LOCAL SCHOOL
MIDDLE SCHOOL LIBRARY

The Wolfman of Beacon Hill

The Wolfman of Beacon Hill

A Novel by
Kathleen Kilgore

Little, Brown and Company
BOSTON   TORONTO

COPYRIGHT © 1982 BY KATHLEEN KILGORE

ALL RIGHTS RESERVED. NO PART OF THIS BOOK MAY BE REPRODUCED IN ANY FORM OR BY ANY ELECTRONIC OR MECHANICAL MEANS INCLUDING INFORMATION STORAGE AND RETRIEVAL SYSTEMS WITHOUT PERMISSION IN WRITING FROM THE PUBLISHER, EXCEPT BY A REVIEWER WHO MAY QUOTE BRIEF PASSAGES IN A REVIEW.

Third Printing

Library of Congress Cataloging in Publication Data

Kilgore, Kathleen.
  The wolfman of Beacon Hill.

  Summary: A teenage runaway and social worker are brought closer together by their shared interest in the fate of an escaped wolf struggling for survival in the streets of Boston.
  [1. Wolves—Fiction. 2. Runaways—Fiction.
3. Boston (Mass.)—Fiction] I. Title.
PZ7.K5548Wo 1982   [Fic]   82–8996
ISBN 0-316-49306-6   AACR2

BP
BOOK DESIGNED BY S. M. SHERMAN

*Published simultaneously in Canada
by Little, Brown & Company (Canada) Limited*

PRINTED IN THE UNITED STATES OF AMERICA

To my mother, Helen Ford Kilgore

The Wolfman of Beacon Hill

1

The voice was high and unforced. The sound drifted through the darkening woods like a boy soprano's descant echoing through the stone ribs of a vast cathedral. But the melody was written in an alien, minor key — sliding up and down through quavering variations no human throat could produce. For a minute, the voice was strong and full. Then it turned down to a final, sad diminuendo, and faded into the night.

The boys sat still for a moment, torn between the feelings the voice had wakened inside them, and their fear of looking foolish in front of their friends.

Then Lucas stood up, crackling the dry leaves under his running shoes, threw back his head, and howled in return. "Yow-woooo!" he shouted in the direction the voice had come from. "Yoo-ooowaaah!"

But there was no answer.

"Hey, listen to *him*!" Jerry shouted. "The Wolfman of Beacon Hill!"

"Hey, Mister Lucas, look at the back of you hands. They all hairy!" Sean giggled.

Jerry cupped his hands before his face and howled too. Then the twins, Sean and Kevin. For a minute, they all howled and laughed.

Kendo, the tall black kid with a shaved head, raised one hand. "Hush," he said softly to Jerry. "Maybe the real Mistah Wolf gon howl agin."

3

The kids, and Lucas, fell silent, sitting around the fire.

To a stranger, they would have seemed an odd grouping. Kendo, tall as a man and straight, a martial arts jacket over his jeans and rubber thongs on his long feet. Jerry, skinny and quick, his hands always moving, the back of his acne-pitted neck sunk into the upturned Barracuta coat collar. Sean and Kevin in identical bowling jackets with *Leprechaun Tap* machine-embroidered on the back, their long hair spilling over white, sad faces.

And Lucas, a long, disjointed figure in track shorts and a Save the Whales T-shirt. His thick brown hair was bushed out in a white man's afro. Yet under the curls and the thick glasses, wrinkles threaded the skin under his eyes.

They waited, but the voice did not sing again.

"Hey, Mister Lucas, you think that's a real wolf?" Sean poked the fire with a stick.

"Yeah. I heard them once when I was up in Alaska. It's beautiful."

"Hey, don't shit us, man, that sucka sounds just like my brother's Malamute." Jerry squirmed to find a comfortable seat on the hard ground. "There ain't no wolves in Massachusetts."

"Yeah, well for your information, this is *Maine*," Sean said.

"Same thing." Jerry spat into the fire. "This ain't the Wild West."

"It was, not too long ago," Lucas said. "This whole area was climax forest when the whites came. Wolves, bear, cougars, the whole scene. Huge trees, dark underneath." He gestured at the scrubby woods around them. "Then they cut the whole thing for firewood and farmed the hell out of it, and it's just now coming back. Those trees probably aren't fifty years old.

"If the forest comes back, the rest of the ecosystem may come back too, if a few animals survived in the hills all these years. They ran a story in the *Globe* last winter, some guy actually photographed cougar tracks in the snow on a logging road up here. If the cougars can make it, why not the wolves?"

"How come you was in Alaska?" Brian asked.

Lucas smiled. The kids, still, after a month, had no concept of his life before Project Turnabout. A social worker was a social worker. Period. In fact this job was his first experience with "human services."

But not theirs.

The kids who wound up at Project Turnabout, Lucas had discovered, knew more about the Department of Social Services than the employees. Some had been placed twenty or thirty times — foster homes paid by the day because the kids couldn't last a week. They knew his salary, and who was a temporary employee, who was civil service, and who had political connections. They knew everything about the system that controlled them. And nothing about anything else.

"I was in Alaska doing a whale census for Greenpeace," Lucas said simply.

A month ago, he would have expected the words "whale," "Greenpeace," or "Alaska" to elicit a flow of questions. But he had discovered that these kids were rarely curious.

They sat around the fire and nodded, tired from the long hike but unused to silence. Lucas had forbidden them their transistors and tape decks.

Kendo sat cross-legged and stared at the big, pollution-red moon, so flat it seemed to hang like a photograph just beyond the line of scrub pines where vision blurred and blackness began. Unlike the others, Kendo seemed to be really listening to the forest sounds: the nighthawk's soft *foop-whoop* call, the shrill of crickets in the heat. From deep in the pines came the sharp note of an owl.

Jerry yawned, stretched his skinny arms, and lay full length on the bedroll.

"Man, this is a bummer," he said.

"Hey, Mister Lucas, you think we oughta sleep?" Brian asked. "I mean, suppose it's a real wolf?"

"If he's survived around here, he's smart enough to leave humans strictly alone." Lucas spread out his bedroll. "They don't mess with people. Any book will tell you that."

"Yeah, but suppose *he* don't read *books*, huh?" Jerry said.

The others laughed.

"Yeah," Sean. "Or s'pose he reads Little Red Riding Hood. Then we *all* dead meat!"

"Everybody's a comedian," Lucas said. "Hey, you guys try and get some sleep, okay? We got a long day tomorrow."

"Yeah. Back to the real world," Brian said.

Kendo stretched his long, taut body on his sleeping bag. "The real world is an il-*lus*ion," he said softly.

Jerry rolled his eyes, but said nothing.

"That's enough talking," Lucas said. "You guys settle down. I'll take care of the fire."

One by one, they yawned and stretched, wriggling their bodies in and out of the hollows of tree roots. Breathing evened, and jaws went slack.

Over the sound of crickets, Jerry began to snore softly.

Lucas sat silent, watching the dying fire. From the pines, an owl called again. But the wolf, if he were nearby, made no sound. Perhaps it was only a dog. How many years had it been, four or five, since Alaska?

Lucas watched them as they slept. They seemed much younger now, crouched fetally like babies. Sean, his yellow hair spread over the forehead, mouthed the knuckle of his thumb.

For a month, Lucas had been their "caregiver" eight hours a day, and usually more. Before the latest round of budget cutting, Project Turnabout had been fully staffed twenty-four hours a day. Now the workers put in eight hours a day, and took turns sleeping at the house. The kids could never be left alone.

The odd hours suited Lucas. Since Barbara had moved out, he had trouble sleeping in the empty Chestnut Street apartment, and the quiet affluence of the neighbors shamed him. Without her salary, Lucas could not have rented a parking space in the Brimmer Street garage, much less a two-bedroom unit in a townhouse. He had been allowed to stay on because the developer didn't want the unit empty until construction began.

Lucas had taken this social service job with vague

memories of his college housefather, a grad student who had let the kids keep beer in his refrigerator and disappeared for long weekends in New York. Lucas had also taken the job before he met the "client population."

Sean and Kevin were fraternal twins. At thirteen, they could read their names, EXIT, and the subway stops on the Red Line but not the Orange. Day and night, they were rarely separated, but rarely in agreement. A hand would steal out and jab a rib cage, or a foot slip behind a leg and jerk, and the two would be rolling, punching, biting, kneeing, knocking over tables, loosening the banisters, pulling lamps down by the cords, slamming doorknobs against the plaster walls. The Dynamic Duo had trashed every bedroom in the house, until the staff gave up and allowed them two mattresses on the floor of a bare room. They slept on one, legs and arms tangled around each other like kittens. When they slept.

Jerry was sixteen. He had taken on the role of wise-ass, but if he left, another kid would step into the part. Jerry's "biologicals" retained some interest in him, and every six months he would pack up his tapes and a pile of clothes in a black plastic trash bag, and be driven away to see relatives. He visited, too, at another foster home. But in a few days he would be back, silent and bitter.

It was Kendo who worried Lucas. There was almost nothing in his files, yet every worker who dealt with him believed the rumors that he was a killer. The story varied —that he had accidentally shot his foster mother, or stabbed somebody's lady in a fight, or that he hanged dogs and cats and torched them. Yet he was literate, and the only kid of the group who could handle public high school. He spent most of his time working out at a storefront karate school, and his room was full of chrome trophies and silken banners. He had been eligible for adoption for five years. No worker would take the case.

In the dim firelight, his dark body was almost invisible as Lucas watched him. Only the white shirt, the belt loosened for sleep, glowed faintly.

Carefully, Lucas banked the fire with loose dirt, brushing away dry leaves and sticks. There was no wind in the still woods, but he had learned to take no chances. Lucas crouched, waiting in the darkness, until the boys were deep in sleep. Then he picked up his flashlight and started down the path.

For a time, Lucas walked with the flashlight picking out details, but soon he switched it off, able to see dimly in the moonlight. He walked toward the pond he had noticed on the way up. The woods still held the damp heat, and he began to sweat again, the T-shirt chafing at his arms.

Clouds passed before the moon for an instant, and Lucas paused. The haze and full moon had obscured all but the brightest stars, and he could recognize none of the familiar constellations.

As the clouds passed again, he caught the glint of water on his left.

Stepping carefully, Lucas walked toward the reeds. Mud welled up in his shoes.

Lucas stripped off his T-shirt, his running shorts, and his jock, spread them over a scrub oak beside his flashlight, and waded into the pond. The marsh grass and dead reeds bit sharp against his flesh, hurrying him in. The water at the edge was warm and soupy, full of clinging weeds.

As the water reached his thighs, Lucas slid in to swim, leaving his head above water like a turtle to keep his glasses dry. Slowly, he side-stroked across, pausing between each kick to lie suspended in the water. The knotted muscles in his shoulders began to loosen.

Swimming at night brought back a thrill of the forbidden. The only deep water near his childhood home had been abandoned stone quarries. Like all the town kids, he had not been allowed to swim there, for almost every summer there was a drowning in the icy water. And, like all the other town kids, he had swum anyway.

Summers were hot in Vermillion, Ohio, the Sandstone Capital of America. Long afternoons passed reading science fiction and Sherlock Holmes, stretched out on the chaise longue in the screened porch. In the evening, there was the thrill of the swim, and then the hot night and the Baby Ben alarm clock ticking on the bedside table, and the train whistle, going on to Cleveland, Chicago, and the West. The train to all the wild places he had never seen.

A fish nibbled Lucas's ankle, and he kicked harder, finishing with the brest stroke. Under his feet, the mud bottom was rising again, and reeds crowded in on him.

Lucas edged himself out of the water and shook himself. The same scrub bushes lined the other side, spotted with blueberry, and, where the ground was damp, a stand of blue monkshood.

Lucas took off his thick glasses and wiped them carefully on a leaf. The scene blurred out of focus. He looked around for a moment with naked eyes. The moon spread into an orange smear; stars turned from pins of light into white blurs. Trees ran together into one black shadow. And, in the midst of the shadows, a patch showed suddenly white.

Lucas put on his glasses and stared at the white. The space resolved itself into a dog: a huge, white German shepherd with long legs. The dog was so close he could almost put a hand out to pat it. But it stood stone still.

Then the animal's eyes told him it was not a dog. The eyes were yellow, shining like a cat's — the dark, round pupils wide. They stared back at Lucas without a dog's submission, but with the cool, appraising glance of an equal. Gray-tipped white fur bristled out around its head like a mane. Only the black nose twitched, judging him by his smell.

Lucas stood just as still, holding his breath while his pulse sang in his eardrums. Along his naked arms, the hairs prickled into gooseflesh. Lucas willed his body not to tremble.

Then the white animal turned and was gone.

2

The howling started as soon as Tony DiNatale put his foot on the old wooden porch steps. The doorbell hadn't worked in years, but the house didn't need one — on any visitor's arrival, the dogs sounded the alarm, jumping and scratching at the glass panels with long toenails. From a broken board under the porch, a yellow striped cat with one ear missing flowed up to Tony and rubbed against his pant leg, hoping to be let in.

Tony stood at the heavy door for a moment. Like the rest of the house, the door was ornately Victorian, and overlaid with coat after coat of alligator-scaled paint. There had once been a screen door, but the metal had bent when someone kicked the plastic panel in. Through the cracks around the glass panels, Tony noticed that the door had once been blue. Now it was a grayed latex white. He gave it a shove.

In the hallway, the German shepherd–Doberman with the bad eye whined and wiggled its haunches, and the new part-Labrador puppy jumped on him, toenails raking his pant leg. Unnoticed, the cat slipped past them and slid under the couch. In the big parlor, a black-and-white television muttered cartoons to empty armchairs.

Tony waited, studying the heap of socks and windbreakers, roller skates, sweaters piled on the floor of the wooden wardrobe in the hallway. The puppy had messed again, in the corner. When he was little, Tony would have said an Our Father for luck under his breath. Ourfatherwhoartinheaven, let the Old Man not be here!

But Tony was not little anymore. He knew that all the prayers in the world would not make the Old Man be away. He held his breath.

"That you, Tony?" the Old Man called from the kitchen.

Tony said nothing. I am strong. I am not afraid, he said in his mind. His foster brother Danny had taught him that. When you're afraid, they can get you.

"Shut the door! You let the hot air in!" the Old Man shouted. Tony could see no difference between the heat of the street and inside, except that inside the dog smell was worse, but he closed it and flipped the deadbolt because the latch was broken.

"Come in here, Tony," the Old Man yelled. "Well, hurry up. I ain't got all day!"

You do. You do got all day, Tony thought, but didn't speak.

In the kitchen, the Old Man sat at the long plastic-topped table, listening to News Radio 59 on a small black transistor. He was drinking coffee from a chipped Red Sox mug. A single sheet of paper lay on the table in front of him, the ashtray and the piles of junk mail pushed aside. The Old Man put down his cigarette and picked up the paper.

"Know what this is?" he asked Tony.

Tony shook his head.

"Don't give me that! You know what it is. Don't you?"

Tony shrugged.

"You signed it! You oughta know what it is! Or can't you read your own writin'? Answer me; You *speak* when I ask you something!"

"Yeah." Tony looked at the linoleum floor. Around the table legs it was thin and dark. "I signed it."

The Old Man read out loud. "Behavior Contract. 'I the young person going into this foster home, a minor, agree to: one, abide by the rules of the people with whom I will live and be subjected to their guidance. Two, be at home at expected times, not staying out overnight without their permission.' You signed that?"

Tony nodded.

"Holy Joseph, will you open your *mouth!*" the Old Man exploded. "Where the hell have you *been* for three days?"

Tony cleared his throat. "Around."

"Around. *Around.* What the hell is *that* supposed to mean?"

"Nothing."

"How the hell do you think you're gonna get a job when all you do is screw *around?* Huh? You wanna be a bum all you life? Answer me!"

Tony stuck his hands in his jeans pockets and stared at the Old Man, taking in the thick folds of skin under his neck, the red stigmata of hypertension across the cheeks and bridge of his nose. He thought of the fat Old Man with Ma, and anger rose up in him.

"How you ever gonna get a job and make a living?" the Old Man shouted. "You ever think about that?"

"You don't work, and you don't do too bad," Tony said suddenly.

The Old Man's eyes narrowed. "I'm on a hundred percent disability," he said slowly. "You think I *like* that? You think I *like* living off a VA check? You think that, you ain't just crazy. You're stupid!"

"You don't look like you got no disability to me," Tony shouted. "You ain't in no wheelchair! You can move your ass down to the barroom any time you feel like it."

"Let me tell you something, you little punk. I'm still more of a man than you'll ever be." The Old Man rose heavily and pushed back the chair.

Tony backed away towards the refrigerator. As he glanced around, he saw that Ma had stuck up his drawing of the dragon fighting the eagle.

"I ain't gonna hit you," the Old Man said softly. "I already called the social worker. You're going to a group home. She won't place you with a family no more. You *understand?* You run one time too many, Tony. You're goin' in with the other punks where you belong."

"You don't have to kick me out, because I'm going anyway," Tony said.

In the hallway, the dogs got up and shook themselves off.

"Hey, you can't just leave like that!" the Old Man yelled after him. "You stay here until your worker comes!"

But Tony was already on the porch steps.

"I'm callin' the cops on you! You hear that?" the Old Man yelled.

Tony turned the corner and began to run, jumping over the breaks in the sidewalk like a horse running downhill.

As he ran, the tension loosened in his belly, and he drank in long breaths of the heavy air.

He ran easily, almost like the men he saw in expensive shoes circling Boston Common, his arms pumping loosely, sneakers *slap slap slap* on the hot pavement. Every step left the Old Man behind. At the corner where the church had been burnt out, he turned towards the trolley stop and began to laugh.

3

The voices sang in chorus. The first came in alone, then another joined a half-tone lower, then a third and fourth until the air was full of continuous high sounds, throbbing and keening up and down the minor scale. Puppy yelps joined in, like children shouting. The voices joined, entangled, twined their melodies around each other, then separated, diminishing.

"FOR CHRISSAKE SHADDUP! SHADDUP!" A human voice broke through. The voices paused for an instant, then began again.

Vinnie Boudreau opened the mobile home door and stood on the wooden porch zipping his fly and tucking his undershirt into his shorts.

"SHADDUP WILLYA, HUH?" he shouted despairingly.

This time there was quiet. In the dawn stillness, the air conditioner in the mobile home window hummed, and the locusts wound up their metal calls in the stand of pines.

In the pen next to the raccoons, the eastern timber wolves settled down to wait for the opening of Animal Forest Park.

Vinnie Boudreau stood blinking in the hot sun and surveyed his domain. At the edge of his vision, a billboard reading "HERDS OF TAME LOOSE ANIMALS TO PET AND FEED — AMUSEMENTS THRILL RIDES — BRING THE WHOLE FAMILY" sagged against a clump of blooming ragweed.

Behind the gate house with the turnstyle and gift shop, asphalt paths wandered through a maze of chain-link pens where animal shapes lay huddled in the sparse shade of a few thin pines and paper birches.

In less than an hour, the tape-recorded calliope music would bellow out of the speakers over the merry-go-round in the neighboring park, shrieking the same ten tunes until the rides closed at midnight. Vinnie knew most of the amusement park people by name, but carny people mostly stuck together. His world was Marie and the animals.

"Why you bother yellin' at those poor dumb animals. huh?" Marie walked onto the porch. She reached her arms around his paunch and squeeezed. Her voice smiled. "You think they understand English or somethin'?"

"Maybe they do. Who knows?" Vinnie put an arm around her shoulder for a moment, then turned away. Secretly, he was ashamed of yelling at the wolves. They hadn't meant to wake him. They were only doing what was natural to them.

Sometimes in the winter he would lie awake and listen to them howl their heads off. He would lie there and imagine them as they ought to be, running free over the snow, under the cold stars. But in the tourist season, when they had to stay penned up, their howling brought him only guilt and anger.

"You want breakfast?" Marie ran her fingers through her thin, coppery dyed hair. The heat had wilted her. In the short shorts and limp tank top, the bulges of fat in her thighs and the knotted blue veins in her legs showed cruelly.

"Nah. Maybe later." Vinnie rummaged under the porch for the fifty-pound bag of Purina Dog Chow. Guy up to Wells had promised him a sick cow, but the vet had pulled her through. The dog chow would have to do.

When Vinnie got close to the wolf pen, he saw why they had been singing. At the mouth of the den the female had dug, the half-grown pups were gnawing on the bones of what had been a turkey. The unmated male was lying on his back nearby, lazily batting a white feather with his huge paw. The white male and his mate lay together contentedly.

"Holy shit," Vinnie said.

The gate was still firmly padlocked. He must have

climbed the fence again. The asphalt kept them from digging under at the edges now, but the white male had learned how to put his paws through the links and go over the top. Vinnie looked up, and saw white feathers clinging to the top strand of barbed wire.

"What happened?" Marie came up behind him.

"He got another turkey," Vinnie said.

"But the barbed wire. How *could* he?"

"Ask him," Vinnie shrugged.

The white wolf's yellow eyes seemed almost to smile at them. Marie shook her head.

"Vinnie, he's got to go," she said. "Can't you see? What else can we do?"

"We've been over this before. You agreed we'd keep him till they get the wilderness park set up. For God's sake, if any captive wolf can make it back to the wild, *he* can. An eight-foot fence with three strands of barbed wire! He is a born *survivor*. They're gonna need his kind of genes in the pack to make it in the wild."

The white wolf yawned luxuriantly, displaying his fangs, as if he knew they were talking about him. His pups began to tussle over a bone, rolling over each other. As always, the top-ranked puppy won.

"Vinnie, there may never *be* a wilderness park. You know that. The hunters and the gun clubs are against it. The governor is against it. All the politicians around here are against it.

"The only people *for* it are a couple of bureaucrats in the Interior Department and those eco-freaks out in Colorado. Even if we do get it, he may be too old by that time. Look, we *know* Franklin Park Zoo will take him. That's for certain."

"It's just another pen. I don't want him in no pen."

"Vinnie, I don't want him penned up either, but what else —"

"You don't care, do you?" he turned on her, his face twisted. "You don't care how any of the animals *feel*, do you? Do you?"

The wolves lay stone still, pricking up their ears.

"Of course I care!" Marie shouted at him. "Do you think I'd stay around this dump if I didn't? Huh?"

The adult wolves rose and paced toward the wire. The female whined nervously.

"See," she choked. "Now you got 'em all upset."

Vinnie shook his head. "I'm sorry," he said dumbly. "I'm sorry." He lowered his voice. "Hey, maybe old man Ritter won't notice one turkey, huh? He must have two, three hundred."

A metal buzzer sounded on a tree trunk next to the mobile home. "I'll get the phone." Marie left him alone with his wolves.

Vinnie entered the pen carefully, not letting any of the wolves squeeze past him. The white wolf came up first to greet him, his right as dominant animal in the pack. He pranced joyously up to Vinnie, then gently grabbed his forearm between his massive jaws and held it gently, his eyes shining. The other wolves bounded and wagged their tails and danced around him in the morning sun, their gray-brown coats glistening as the light glanced off the varied colors.

Vinnie scratched the white wolf behind the ears. "You old sonofabitch," he murmured. "What am I gonna do with you, huh?" Then he bent down to scratch first the unmated male, the female, and at last the pups, sticking to their pack order.

When Marie came out of the trailer, her face was gray.

Vinnie stiffened. Instantly, the wolves backed off.

"What's the matter?" Vinnie asked. But he already knew.

"That was Ritter. He didn't take just one turkey. He got the gate open somehow and chased the whole flock into the woods. Two hundred odd. They're trying to round them up now."

For a moment, Vinnie smiled at the thought of old red-faced Ritter trying to round up two hundred stupid, panicky turkeys.

"He got the sheriff to swear out a warrant half an hour ago," she said.

Vinnie unlatched the gate and stepped out. "When is he coming?" he asked thickly.

"Any time now."

Vinnie swallowed. "I got three-quarters of a tank in the camper. I'll run him down to Franklin Park now. You explain when he gets here. Don't let him near the others, you understand?"

"Don't you want something to eat?" Marie asked.

"I ain't hungry," Vinnie said.

Vinnie walked through the park to the shed where he kept his tools. The animals were more active now, waiting for feeding time. Marie would have to take care of that.

Over his head, the capuchin monkey slid down the wire suspended between two trees, his chain rattling. Vinnie passed under quickly — the monkey had taken to peeing on people from his perch, and something would have to be done about it.

A couple of rank-smelling billy goats trotted out to Vinnie and nudged his pockets. The white-tailed deer nosed at him briefly as he passed their enclosure.

As the sun pierced under the tree branches, the stink rose around Vinnie like fog. No matter how many times he hosed down the asphalt and mucked out the cages, it always smelled. Vinnie glanced at the chimpanzee in the enclosure behind the shed. It hunched in a corner, its back turned to Vinnie.

"Serves you right," Vinnie shouted at it, venting his anger. He had paid four hundred dollars for a female, and the chimp had killed her the first day! Maybe he had been in captivity too long and didn't know what to do, Vinnie realized. But still the memory bothered him.

Vinnie found the wolf's choke collar hanging on a peg, and his pain stabbed at him. He grabbed a length of rope, slammed the door shut, and ran back to the wolf pen.

When he saw the chain, the white wolf bounded out the gate, wriggling with pleasure. In winter when the park was closed, Vinnie used to take him out to the fields and let him play in the snow. But now those days were gone.

As Vinnie slipped the chain on, the white wolf stood up

on his hind legs and braced his paws on Vinnie's shoulders. The wolf's massive head was now level with his own. The wolf gently touched his face, licking him with quick, gentle flicks of the tongue. The animal's tongue was rough and hot.

Vinnie's vision clouded. "Get offa me, you big slob." He tried to put annoyance in his voice, but the wolf was not fooled. "Leave me alone, willya?"

The wolf followed Vinnie eagerly to the camper. With a graceful leap, he dove through the side window into the passenger seat and sat expectantly, his tongue hanging out.

Vinnie yanked the door open. "You gotta ride in the back this time," he told the wolf. He pulled at the rope, and the wolf jumped down and allowed himself to be led to the rear. Vinnie guided him into the dark compartment.

Once the camper had held two foam-rubber beds with covers that matched the curtains Marie had made for the windows, but over the years the space had filled with old garden hose, screening, gasoline cans, extra fence posts, half-empty cans of paint. It would be hot as hell in there on the highway, but the wolf had shed his heavy coat in the spring, and the fall hair hadn't begun to come in. Besides, Vinnie told himself, the white wolf was a born survivor.

Vinnie tied the rope securely onto one of the bed fixtures, filled a bucket half full of water, and wedged it into a corner where the wolf could reach it. As he jumped down, the wolf rose to his feet to follow, but Vinnie slammed the door.

For a moment, the wolf thrashed desperately about,

knocking over the water pail and tearing at the metal walls with his claws. Then, just as suddenly, he stopped and stood panting in the darkness. He crouched down between a bicycle tire and a roll of chicken wire, closed his eyes, and waited.

4

At the trolley stop, Tony checked the newspaper machine. It was empty. He shrugged, kicked at the metal plate along the bottom. Early in the morning, he could have emptied the machine for a quarter and sold the papers at Mister Donut. Now it was nearly noon. Even if the machine were full, people would be looking for the afternoon edition. He kicked the metal again.

On the rough concrete behind him, someone had carefully painted a red swollen tongue protruding from a leering mouth. Other kids had hastily scrawled things as a sign of their passing: "Denise loves Kevin" with the "loves" crossed out, and "sucks on" written over; "Dorchester Rules"; "Party till you puke"; "Mattapan Projects #1"; Nazi emblems, cult names. Tony kicked a Tab can and sent it spinning onto the gravel around the rail.

His mouth tasted acid now, and the walls of his stomach

seemed to cling together like Saran wrap. How long had it really been, Tony wondered? He had heard about people fasting for weeks, months, starving themselves to protest something. What was the matter with him that he couldn't go one lousy day without a meal?

Tony spat the sour taste onto the asphalt. There was still no trolley. Bits of broken glass and metal glittered in the gravel along the tracks.

"Hey, what's happenin', man?" Brian came up behind him.

"The Old Man," Tony shrugged. "I split."

"Hey, no shit?" Brian laughed. "For how long, two minutes?" Brian laughed again. 'He call the rollers on you, huh?" Brian flipped open a box pack of Camels and offered one to Tony.

"Yeah, he called the cops."

"Hey, I bet you really scared, man?" Brian laughed harshly. "I bet that's the number-one priority nine-eleven call over to Station Eleven. Runaway kid in Dorchester! Jeeesus, I bet that's right up there with dumping on state property and parking in a tow zone! I bet you hit the Crimes of the Week list at Berkeley Street."

"Yeah, I'm really shakin'." Tony took a deep drag on the unfiltered cigarette and coughed.

"Hey, maybe they get the Litter Patrol on your case," Brian laughed. "Dum de dum dum," he hummed the theme song from *Dragnet*. "My name's Friday. I'm a Litter Patrolman. I pick up dogshit."

Tony didn't laugh.

"Wanna bit o' horny?" Brian leered at the last word.

Tony took the candy eagerly and held it in his mouth, feeling the sugar ease the twisting in his stomach.

"Hey, Tony, do me a favor, huh?" Brian said after a while.

"What?"

"Go back home. I seen your ma. She's a nice lady, know what I mean? She been too nice to you — now you too na-eeve for the street."

"I ain't goin' back to *him*," Tony said.

"What he do?" Brian asked, shifting from foot to foot like a fighter. "What he do, break your arm? Hold your hand over the gas stove, shit like that? What he do?"

"No, none of that stuff."

"You got food. You got shoes, you got nice shoes, Tony. Nikes." He glanced at Tony's feet. "New Nikes. You know what Nikes cost, Tony?"

"They pay him. The social worker pays him, and he pisses it away on beer."

"Tony, man, this is *summer*. It ain't like this alla time. You go onna street in January, you gonna know you are onna *street*. How you gonna paint your pretty pictures onna street?"

"I can take it."

"You dumb asshole Ginny," Brian said sadly. "You don't shoot stuff in your arm, you got no record at Youthie, so what you doin' onna street? Go home."

Tony spat the taste of cigarette onto the asphalt. An old woman with a Star Market shopping bag edged warily away from him toward the concrete overhang. Tony realized, uneasily, that she feared him. He shook his head and spat again. Tony was used to being afraid — he was small for his age and too nervous to be a good fighter — but he was not used to being feared. The small feeling of power gave him no pleasure.

"You stink, Brian, you know that?" Tony said suddenly.

Brian hitched up his jeans, pulling up the rolled-up cuffs that had frayed and grown black from rubbing against the street. Tony wanted to wear his jeans rolled too, but Ma always got hold of them and hemmed them.

"You gonna stink too, you sleep where I do," Brian said, unperturbed. "Go home, baby," he added.

The trolley car creaked to a stop before them. Tony and Brian pushed on ahead of the other passengers and scuttled to the rear.

The old trolley was double-headed, and once could have been driven from either end, but now the abandoned rear driver's seat was stripped to its black iron frame. Trash had been wedged around the disused fare box. Tony and Brian perched themselves around the seat and braced for the trolley driver to release the brakes.

"I could take him out easy," Brian said, gesturing toward a young Chinese kid. "But Chinks ain't got shit."

"Yeah, the Japs have all the bread." Tony nodded wisely.

The trolley rattled along through a cemetery. Tony felt better now; the sensation of moving, going somewhere, gave him courage.

He read a bank ad: "What this Country needs is Guaranteed Freedom and Security." Someone had crossed out "Freedom and Security," and written "A Revolution!" Tony opened his mouth to point it out to Brian, then remembered Brian could not read.

Instead of reading the signs, Brian was reading the passengers. His cigarette held low beneath his bent knee, he gazed at each one, not meeting their eyes. Nothing promising this time of day: old women, a couple of young mothers with kids on their way to the Welfare Office on Adams Street, black kids — Brian never messed with blacks — four dummies from the halfway house on the state hospital grounds and their attendant, a bearded man with a ponytail. The dummies were laughing and pointing, thrilled with the hot, dirty car.

At the last stop, Tony and Brian scooted the length of the trolley, slipped out ahead of the rest, and ducked under the subway turnstile while the others lined up at the booth to buy tokens. The starter watched them, and said nothing.

"Common?" Tony asked their destination.

Brian nodded, flicking his cigarette expertly into the black hole where the subway train would come.

5

"Live Free or Die! Bienvenue au/Welcome to New Hampshire." Vinnie thought he could hear the wolf moving in the camper behind him as he dropped his forty cents into the basket, but it might have been the junk shifting around. He accelerated into the middle lane under the sign for Hampton Boston 95 South.

The road was full of vacationers: huge blimp-shaped motor homes; old Fords pulling flat trailers that folded into tents; Plymouth station wagons crammed with Styrofoam coolers and buckets and dogs, bare kid feet sticking up in the windows; Volvos with white plastic cases that looked like giant Big Mac containers strapped to the tops and ten-speed bicycles fastened to the rear.

On every trip it seemed to Vinnie that there were fewer farms and more factories. Where the land was still open, the old stands of corn and hayfields were grown over with red-tipped sumac bush, or in boggy spots, bright purple loosestrife was dotted with goldenrod.

Vinnie drove in the middle lane, letting the semis and the Greyhound buses pass him by — one browned arm resting on the windowframe, and the other hand in his lap, holding the bottom of the steering wheel with two fingers.

The time of year always made Vinnie feel a touch of sadness, the way most people felt at the first signs of fall. In the height of summer, he read the signs of its death:

the insect sounds, the end of birdsong, the young animals suddenly striking out on their own, and the old ones foraging to build up a layer of fat. The season changes seemed to come so much faster now, or was that only a sign that he himself was growing old?

At the next border (NEW MASS. GUN LAW MANDATORY SENTENCE FOR VIOLATION ONE YEAR!), the suburbs began. Vinnie tightened his grip on the wheel as a semi passed him loaded with wrecked cars, squashed flat as though a giant had stomped them, rattling in their chains. His ordeal had begun.

The highway narrowed as the buildings crowded in, so that to Vinnie it felt like being sucked down a drain. First motels and truck dealers, mobile home parks sprouting forests of antennae, Body Shop, Puritan Lawn Park Cemetery Visitors Welcome. Then the signs elbowed in closer like high palings. Pancakes Family Fare, Carpet World, Health Spa, Green Apple Entertainment Nitely All New Girls, Meat World, Piggy's Pizza — the Best Piece in Town.

Vinnie kept to the middle lane while the roads merged around him into one, all headed for the blue haze over the city towers.

The camper paused at the top of the bridge over the Mystic River tank farms while Vinnie paid the toll. Then it shot into the maze of overpass girders that led to downtown.

10:21, the bank sign read. *Temperature 89 F*. The air burned his eyes.

Just at the Atlantic Avenue turnoff, the wheel began to

stiffen under his hand. Vinnie signaled to turn right. He pulled at the wheel, braking hard, but the camper would not respond. Horns blared behind him. As he slowed, he heard the right front tire thumping against the pavement, and knew what the trouble was.

More horns. Cars swerved and veered around him. Sweating, Vinnie turned on the flashers, and the camper limped over to the curb. Vinnie eased himself across the seat and out of the cab on the passenger side. The tire was dead flat, a long chunk of metal still wedged in through the tread like a knife in cheese. Then Vinnie remembered that the spare and the jack were somewhere in back with the wolf.

Vinnie edged around to the back on the curb side through the cacophony of horns and shouting, his eyes tearing from the heat and traffic fumes, and wrenched open the camper's rear door.

He felt a tap on his shoulder and spun around, panicked.

"Hey, take it easy, fella." Vinnie stood facing a gray-haired man in a sweat-blackened Boston Police uniform. "You need some help?"

Dimly, Vinnie saw the other cop waving traffic away. The cruiser, lights flashing, was parked directly behind him.

"I got a spare in here!" Vinnie shouted over the noise.

"Fine. I'll help you."

"No, no wait —" Vinnie shouted, but the man had already vaulted into the door. Vinnie's heart seemed to stop as the man stared at the white shape crouching in the corner.

But the man only smiled. "Siberian husky, is he?" the cop yelled.

Vinnie nodded.

"Fine-looking dog. Where's your spare?"

Vinnie breathed again. "In back here. Be careful. He ain't real friendly with strangers," he warned. As he searched in the dim light for the spare, Vinnie reached out one hand to check the wolf's collar. The rope was still knotted to the chain, and secured to the camper frame.

Vinnie didn't check the rest of the rope, or find the place near the middle where the wolf had gnawed anxiously at it, alone in the heat and darkness.

As Vinnie gathered up the pieces of the jack, the cop looked appraisingly at the wolf. "You're a real fine animal, there, ain't you, boy?" he spoke soothingly to the wolf. "What's his name?" The cop crouched down next to the wolf.

Suddenly, Vinnie was at a loss. None of his animals had names. Vinnie was a farmer's son, and on his farm you didn't name the stock. You get too attached to them. His father's cows had only numbers.

With the wolves, somehow it would have belittled them to give them human names. They were complete in themselves.

"What's his name?" the cop asked again.

Desperate, Vinnie searched his mind. "Fred," he said at last, thinking of a neighbor's coon dog. "His name's Fred."

"Good dog, Fred. There, you like me, don't you, Fred?" he crooned. "I've always been good with animals," he smiled. "Just born that way."

"Hey, mister, don't —"

But the cop had already reached out to scratch the wolf's ears. A low whining moan grew in the wolf's throat. The ears flattened against his skull, and his body coiled tense and quivering.

"Easy —" Vinnie began, but the wolf had sprung. He leaped past them for the open doorway. The rope held for an instant, then split open. Vinnie grabbed at the nearest coil, but it fell limp at his feet. He heard the wolf's toenails scrabbling on the aluminum steps.

Vinnie shoved the cop aside and jumped out the camper door onto the curb, but the wolf had picked his way between the stalled cars and crossed the street. The flash of white disappeared behind a parked delivery van.

Vinnie stood staring blankly at the cars. The wolf was gone.

"Hey, don't worry," the cop reassured him. "He's got a tag, right? He's just scared now, that's all."

Vinnie's mind felt drugged into torpor, like the dreams he used to have of trying to run but finding his feet wouldn't move. He tried to force himself to think. Should he chase on foot? No, any dog can outrun a man. Chase him in the camper? But it had a flat.

Tell the police the truth? No, that was the worst thing. They would come from all over with guns to kill the white male or anything that looked like him. He knew how people in a small town felt about the wolves, and they lived close to animals. What would city people think?

"He did have a tag, didn't he? You get them with the rabies shot."

Vinnie nodded dumbly.

"No sweat. The Animal Protection League will pick him up. He'll be easy to spot."

Slowly, as if moving caused him immense pain, Vinnie climbed up into the camper and picked up the pieces of the jack.

Tony picked his way from the Park Street exit through the pretzel sellers, musicians, ice-cream carts, beggars. In the middle of a crowd of small children a spider monkey on a chain took coins in its tiny hand, ritually touched a red cap strapped on with a piece of elastic, and handed the coin to its owner. Toward the old information kiosk, now deserted, the Hare Krishna people had laid out an oriental rug and their exotic instruments. The throb of their chant made a counterpoint to the old Irish accordionists next to the newspaper stand.

In the thick of the crowd, a white-haired man, permanently stooped, stood patiently with a cardboard sign wrapped in cellophane hung around his neck: ABORTION IS MURDER! He smiled gently at each passerby, as if he had run into a close friend by chance, and patted the smallest children on the head.

None of this interested Brian. "You wanna check out the Arcade?" he asked.

"Sure. Why not?" Tony looked longingly at a vendor laying mustard on a hotdog with a squeeze bottle, like toothpaste. A tall man whizzed by him on black boot roller skates.

"Hey, lookit the size of that dog, willya?" Tony

pointed at a big white animal loping along the sidewalk. It rushed blindly into the middle of Tremont Street for a moment, then froze, car horns blaring at it.

"I seen bigger dogs than that at D Street Project," Brian said, unimpressed. "Wild ones."

"He's scared," Tony said. For an instant, Tony thought of the strays Ma had taken in, the frightened eyes, the heads hanging low. Then he pushed the thought away.

"He ain't gonna live long if he can't cross the street," Brian shrugged.

The animal bolted back again to the sidewalk, tongue lolling, and dashed around the corner of the building that had once been R. H. Stearns Department Store.

"You hungry?" Brian asked suddenly.

Tony smelled the heavy meat-grease odor as the door of Burger King swung open. "Is the Pope a Catholic?" he asked. "Does a bear shit in the woods?"

"Does the Pope shit in the woods?" Brian laughed.

Tony followed him down the new brick street toward the pedestrian mall between Filene's and Jordan's. They passed a cop on horseback surrounded by children patting the horse's flanks. Tony ducked past a delivery truck, following Brian down the street behind Filene's basement. A crowd of middle-aged shoppers stood near the entrance, rearranging their bundles.

"Keep your eyes open and your mouth shut," Brian said.

6

All day, Vinnie drove the camper or walked through the side streets and the alleys, calling. The wolf would not answer to a name, but should, Vinnie thought, recognize his voice and scent. The wolf was scared, he reasoned, and not likely to run far.

Toward evening, the gas gauge registered on *E*, and Vinnie parked it near the Atlantic Avenue overpass and went on foot. As he walked, downtown shifted its population from the day to the night people. The girls in swirling skirts and backless heels and men in summer suits gave place to the old men in torn overcoats and old women with paper shopping bags full of junk.

All along lower Washington Street, the lights of the bars and porno shops came on, and white Lincoln Continental Mark IVs with wire wheels and extended bodies dropped off girls, then drove slowly around the block. Vinnie walked fast, almost as scared of the lights, the sounds, and the hot greasy smells as the wolf must be.

Then the first rain fell in thick, hard drops. Cool wind rushed down the streets, blowing the dirty papers in eddies. The sidewalk blackened, and rain came in gusts. Vinnie pulled his cap down and ran for the camper.

For a long time he stood at the open door, watching the wet street. Then he went inside and lay on one bare bunk, feeling the coolness wash over him. The rain bounced and fell like shot on the metal roof. He listened to it, numb, not letting himself despair, or hope.

The wolf waited for a long time. All day he had lain behind an abandoned dumpster, drooling and quivering in the heat. With darkness, he ventured out — sniffing, walking a few steps, then flattening himself onto the pavement. The air teemed with smell: sweat, sugar, urine, grease, asphalt, soap, perfume, meat, leather, pigeon, cat, paper, human and animal wastes. Man smell and animal smells he knew, but here every corner was layered with thousands of conflicting scents, overwhelming him. He could read nothing but his own fear.

At first, he crept toward the camper and crouched a few feet away while the rain matted down his coat. But as he saw the open door, new panic swept through him. Fear of the trap. He was the child of only those wolves who were wary of men and traps; trusting wolves left no children. The years with Vinnie had softened those fears, but they rose up now, driving him back.

Several times he crept on his belly close to the narrow black hole that Vinnie's smell came from. Then he retreated, trembling and moaning. Cars swirled by, splattering his long guard hairs with oil and mud. The wolf crept back along the muddy street, stretched himself under a parked car, and waited.

7

Almost a hundred years ago, when steamships came into the port of Boston with wool from Australia and cotton from the South for the mills in Lowell and Lawrence and Manchester, the brick building had been a warehouse full of burlap-wrapped bales, the air thick with lint. As the mills of Lowell and Lawrence and Manchester closed down, the street became a block of garment shops, and the building housed a leather coat factory where illegal Chinese immigrants sweated piecework twelve hours a day, their children playing on the floors.

In the late 1960s a painter looking for space to set up the huge abstractions his clients bought for bank lobbies rented the top floor for $90 a month with no improvements, D.C. wiring, and the only running water a john, next to the outer wall, that froze in February.

Six months later, a sculptor moved downstairs, scraped off the layers of dark varnish with twelve gallons of Stripeeze, and painted the huge spaces white. Across the street, two women set up a shop selling macrame and knitting supplies. Then on the corner came the first restaurant, with Boston ferns suspended in the high windows and the inside walls stripped to old brick.

Ten years after the first painter moved in, the first developer bought the building and began the process to evict the painter. The painter countersued for housing code violations. The developer charged that the painter and the sculptor were illegally sleeping in a nonresidential building. The building was never developed, and after the suits had been two years in court, the other empty spaces inside began filling up at night. First, old men. Then kids.

A year had passed since the developer filed for bankruptcy. Sometimes police, responding to the calls of the condominium owners across the street, would sweep through with flashlights and shove the residents — kids and artists alike — out into the street.

When the police were gone, the sculptor would detach the new front door lock with a bolt cutter, and go back to bed.

At the back of the second floor, in what had been the cotton dealer's office, two boys lay sprawled on an old mattress next to a new plywood partition, built when the developer had begun to convert to condominiums. Piles of wallboard with penciled numbers lay undisturbed, though the lumber had long since been stolen. The rough floorboards were white with a fine dust, printed with the marks of sneaker soles.

Tony sat up and pressed his back against the chalky white wall, his knees drawn up against his stomach. He wanted to throw up again, but the fear of the dark alleyway behind the building was more powerful than nausea. They had dragged the mattress as far as possible away from the blocked-up toilet, but the smell still reached him in the still, hot air. The powder in Brian's joint had dried up his nose and mouth, and chilled his hands and feet, but it could not block out the smell.

It was the rats Tony feared. In his half-dreams he saw

their little red eyes behind the dumpster. The cat at home brought them in whole and wet and slick as a greased D.A. and laid them on the porch. The mice she ate headfirst, and chewed the heads methodically off grass snakes, spitting and yowling if you came too close. But rats she left whole. Were they poison?

Why didn't the cats here kill the rats? Were the cats better at home?

If he asked Brian he would say it was a shitass question. And Brian was asleep, his mouth open, snoring like an old woman.

Through the huge blank windows came the first flickers of lightning. Tony pressed his knees tighter, pushing against the pain. The beginnings of a breeze drifted through the window somebody had wrenched the plywood from, stirring the dead air.

The cat at home. Tony mouthed the word. *Home*.

There really was no such place. Tony's legal father was the Department of Social Services of the Commonwealth of Massachusetts. Tony liked to joke about that — "See that thing on top of the golden dome?" He pointed to the spire on the shining roof of the State House. "That's really a giant prick."

The giant golden prick paid $61.53 a week — when the check was not late — to whomever it delegated as Tony's family. There had been seven mothers and fathers since the day he was removed, on an anonymous complaint, from the top floor of a triple-decker in Revere, near the dog track.

"Maybe your old man was a dog," his friends used to joke. "Or else your old lady was a bitch."

Then Tony would hit out blindly. But Tony was not good with his fists; he was small, and too easily roused to emotion.

Tony had walked in and out the doors of seven homes with seven different workers, called fourteen total strangers "Mom and Dad," and been beaten up by twenty-three new siblings. Ma was, on the whole, one of the best mothers. She was a screamer, but Tony liked the screamers better than the cold ones who said nothing, turning their backs on you to scrub the stove clean. She even liked his pictures. But Ma was married to the Old Man.

Tony stood up unsteadily, slightly bent, his arms clenched around his stomach. He let the image of Ma flood into his mind.

The MBTA shut down at midnight, but it couldn't be more than five, six miles away through South Boston, relatively safe territory for a white kid, if he knew what he was doing. He had walked it a couple of times in daylight when he didn't have carfare.

Damp air gusted through the empty windowframe, smelling like wet leaves on the back porch. Then lightning tore the sky. Tony drew back, gently straightening himself up.

A gust of wind brought rain spattering through the windowframe again, soaking the floorboards. Then it came harder; the storm had come back.

Tony stared for a long time at the waves of water slashing against the streetlight and rebounding off the pavement below. Then, slowly, he eased himself onto the corner of the mattress again, sliding his buttocks to a dent where there were no holes in the gray ticking. He drew his knees up to his chest and closed his eyes.

When it was nearly dawn, the wolf eased his body under the bumper of the car and slid out onto the sidewalk. The cars were fewer now, and the rain had dwindled to a warm mist hazing rainbows around the yellow anti-crime lights.

The wolf stood up and shook himself. For the first time in his life, he was achingly hungry.

Keeping in the shadowed side of the street, the wolf nosed cautiously through the empty textile district — drawn by the food smells of Chinatown, but fearful of the neon lights and noise. On the sidewalk next to a department store, he chewed up a greasy hamburger wrapper, but the taste only intensified his hunger.

At the corner, he caught the faint familiar scent of pigeon. Looking up, he smelled trees, asphalt, trash, and, for a moment, the scent signaled "home." But a deep breath disabused him. Still, the familiar things drew him on. He trotted across the street, tail higher, still trembling, and flattened himself under a park bench.

Down the path came a tall bearded man whistling and tugging at a leash. At the end of the leash stood a gray dog with a coat like a Brillo pad, as big as the wolf. From her thick steamy coat drifted the warm, sweet cheesy smell of bitch close to heat. The bitch stiffened for a moment, ears pricked, as the wolf's strange scent reached her.

"For Jasus's sake, hurry it up, can't you?" the man shouted impatiently. "Bad girl, Rosheen!" he jerked on the lead.

The bitch turned around and nervously defecated on the wet grass.

The wolf waited until they were out of sight. Then he sniffed at the dung until his mind was saturated with its fragrance. With his shoulders down, he rubbed himself in it, rolling over and over until his coat was smeared with her scent.

He waited until the man and dog were nearly out of sight. Then, cautiously, still nervous, he began to track them.

8

Tony blinked and sighted carefully through the crosshairs. Slowly, he sucked in his breath and squeezed the trigger, keeping the barrel level. There was a metallic explosion. The tiger vanished, and digital numbers formed themselves on the glossy screen, then it turned dead gray-green. Tony smiled.

"You're pretty good with that thing, aren't you?" Brian's friend smiled as Tony stuck his head up. Above them, a snarling tiger in neon blinked off and on under the sign TIGER RANGE.

Tony nodded.

"Where did you learn how to shoot?" the man asked him.

"Around," Tony shrugged. He glanced at the man's smooth, white face and neat mustache. It was a pleasant face, didn't come on strong. He wore a softly expensive pink shirt with lime green pants, a linen jacket thrown over one shoulder.

"Let's see you try it again." He handed Tony more quarters.

Tony shrugged. "It's okay, Mr. Bertoli."

"Call me Al." The man smiled again. "Come on, you're just getting warmed up."

Bertoli slipped the quarters into the slot, and Tony bent eagerly to the game again. Over his head, his two friends smiled at each other. The cool, stale air in the Amusement Center was full of the shrieks and pings of the games, like the sound effects for a science fiction film. Smiling, Bertoli focused his eyes on the Dolly Parton pinball machine next to the lunch counter. "He's good," he mouthed at Brian.

Brian rubbed his thumb and first three fingers together slowly.

"Later," Bertoli mouthed.

"Now!" Brian whispered just under the noise. "Now or nothing. *Nada, hombre*."

Still smiling, Bertoli reached into his shirt pocket and

drew out new, folded bills. Brian flipped his finger over the edge, and, satisfied, stuffed the wad into his pants.

"I got a free game," Tony said, excited.

"Hey, great! What'd I tell you, huh?" Bertoli smiled.

Tony bent to the game again. When he looked up, Brian was gone. Tony searched the room with his eyes, suddenly nervous.

Bertoli took him gently by the shoulder. "You don't need him, Tony," he said.

Tony nodded.

"Come on, let's get outa here, okay?" Bertoli asked.

"Sure, okay."

Tony followed him into the hot afternoon sun. In the shop window next to the arcade, frilly women's underwear was displayed: push-up bras and garter belts. On one dummy, the plastic nipples protruded through small holes in a black lace bra. Tony paused, his hands suddenly cold.

Catching his gaze, Bertoli laughed out loud. "For Christ's sake, it isn't like *that*, Tony." He laughed again. "Believe me, it'll be okay. Trust me."

Bertoli flipped open a gold cigarette case and offered it to Tony.

"Everybody's nervous at first. Believe me, there's worse ways to make a living. I should know."

The two walked together along the hot brick pavement, close but not touching.

"How about some new clothes, Tony?" Bertoli asked. "You into that?"

Tony took a deep drag on his cigarette and stopped in

front of a five and dime. The window was filled with afro wigs on gold stands, glittering in the brassy sun. A mounted policeman jingled by them, light glinting on the horse's coat.

"I don't think I can do this, Mr. B.," Tony said softly.

"Like I said, everybody's nervous at first, Tony."

"I mean, it just ain't my thing. I'd screw up." Tony reddened; "I mean, I'd mess up. I mean, I wouldn't be able to go through with it. I mean, it's gross."

Bertoli nodded. "See that car?" He pointed to a white Porsche drawn up at the curb. "That's my car, Tony. I didn't grow up in a fancy neighborhood, Tony. I was like you. My old man was a shoe worker, when he was working, which wasn't too often. But I learned a few things, Tony.

"I learned a couple of things about America. Maybe it's different someplace else, but here you got to pay for what you get. You got to sell what somebody else wants to buy. It's that simple. So tell me, Tony, what else do you have to sell?"

Tony said nothing.

"Nobody's gonna hurt you, Tony. I promise you that, okay?"

Tony did not answer.

"Someday you're gonna have a nice car like that too. If you want it. Do you want it, Tony?"

For an instant on the hot street, Tony pictured in his mind the white car drawn up at the curb near Ma's house. In his mind, he pressed the shiny chrome handle and opened the heavy door, the inside smelling of saddlesoap and leather.

"Yeah, I want it," he whispered.

"Can you drive, Tony? I bet you can."

"Yeah, a little."

"You like to drive it sometime, out in the country?"

Tony nodded.

"Come on, let's get you some decent clothes." Bertoli smiled. "You like those shirts with the little alligators?"

"Yeah. And I need some shoes."

Laughing, Bertoli steered him through the heavy glass doors of Jordan Marsh.

As the shadows lengthened, the wolf edged from under the dumpster in the alley behind The Greenery Natural Foods Restaurant and Plant Boutique. In front of him stood a male German shepherd with his tail carried high. They stared for a moment, brown eyes and yellow, their heads almost level.

The German shepherd lowered his head and spread his front legs wide in a gesture of submission the wolf understood. Slowly, the wolf paced forward and brought his nose to meet the other's nose. They smelled briefly, then wheeled around, the shepherd presenting his anus to be sniffed first.

The shepherd slowly wagged his tail, but the wolf held his brush straight and high. Throwing his weight onto his massive hindquarters, the wolf threw one leg over the shepherd's shoulders while the shepherd crouched, twisting his neck to bare the jugular to the wolf's incisors. They held position for a moment, as though posing for a formal portrait. Then with a lordly toss of his head, the wolf released him.

They stood side by side for a moment in the coolness, then the shepherd trotted to the entrance of an alleyway. The wolf hesitated for an instant, and followed.

The wolf and dog headed down the steep sidewalk together, keeping in the shade of the buildings. Other dogs were roaming free now, let out of the house as their owners came home. A collie bounded down the marble steps of one brick building, a pair of Dobermans with choke collars from another. A St. Bernard, already panting in the heat, sniffed them abruptly as they passed.

Emboldened by his encounter with the shepherd, the wolf drank in the early evening smells of man, dogs, cats, human food from the open windows; garbage, rats, and the faint whiff of skunk and raccoon from the back alleys.

The sidewalk was alive with animal life: pigeons courting, sparrows flicking down to pick seeds from the police horse manure. Every tree and post was saturated with layers of individual scents. Squirrels flowed across the asphalt toward the Common, tails rippling with speed.

At the side of an apartment building, the wolf and dog found a puddle from the drip of an air conditioner. They drank, the wolf first, then lay side by side, scratching and dozing in the warmth.

After a time, the shepherd rose, shook himself, and led the wolf off again. In the alleyway behind an antique shop, they found black plastic garbage bags stacked beside two trash cans. Seizing a bag in his jaws, the shepherd dragged it over the cobblestones, worrying it with his teeth.

The wolf followed, watching. With a quick slash of his incisors, the shepherd tore the plastic apart. Crouching, the wolf fed first, on a crust of pizza, and then stepped aside to let the shepherd share the "kill": stale doughnuts, potato skins, a rotten avocado, white fat trimmed from a steak. They licked the trays of TV dinners until the aluminum shone.

The wolf lay down with an orange juice can full of solidified bacon fat between his front paws and worked his tongue into it, licking the inside clean.

Abruptly, the dog's ears stood up, and he jumped to his feet, tail curving sharply. The wolf followed.

On the bottom step of a brick townhouse, a man stood clapping his hands and whistling.

The shepherd bounded forward and hurled himself against the man, wriggling his hindquarters and barking with joy. The man rubbed the animal's ears and spoke. Silently, the wolf melted back into the alleyway alone. He lay down to wait, still hungry.

As darkness came, the streets began to empty again. Dogs vanished inside doors. Pigeons roosted in the cornices, fluffing their feathers against the cooler temperatures, and church bells rang again. The cycle of the day was ending.

The wolf rose again and drifted slowly out into the street. He scented another large dog and paused. A black

Afghan bitch, recently spayed, with a rhinestone collar, trotted unconcernedly up to him.

The wolf stood still, his nostrils drinking in her odd scent. The smell of hospital disinfectant still clung to the underside of her body where the fur was shaven, and a long scar threaded her gray skin between her black button teats. The wolf sniffed uneasily, staring at her.

But the bitch walked right up, ignoring his uncertainty. She craned her neck to reach his nose. The wolf drew back, affronted, flattening his ears, and waited for her to present her anus. Instead, she reached out and licked him on the mouth, a puppy's gesture.

Swiftly, the wolf spun around and shouldered her down into the proper submission pose. But instead of showing her belly and neck, she yelped and righted herself. Again, the wolf threw her down, using his jaws as well. This time, the bitch whined nervously and snapped at his shoulder, her teeth closing hard on the folds of skin.

With a quick sideways motion, the wolf laid her throat open.

There was no sound. The bitch's head hung limp, and the feet moved convulsively for a moment while her blood pumped from the severed arteries onto the pavement.

The wolf stood still over the dead bitch for a moment, as though unsure what to do next. Then he seized the carcass by the scruff of skin at the neck and dragged it into the alley. Easing his front legs down, he ripped open the thin skin at the belly, spilling the intestines on the asphalt, and ate.

Tony detached the butt from the owl-shaped roach clip and dropped it into the toilet bowl. It spiraled down the smooth porcelain, and was gone. Tony stared at the unfamiliar image in the full-length mirror: navy blue blazer with brass buttons, a clean striped shirt soft against his skin, gray flannel pants. His hair was clean and neatly trimmed, and shone glossy black as a combed racehorse, yet the skin seemed fair now in the pink bathroom light. The new leather shoes pinched his left big toe.

On the shelf over the sink stood a large jar of Vaseline and a box of scented Kleenex.

Tony's chest was hot and itchy under the wool, but his hands were numb with cold.

"Come on, Tony" — Bertoli's voice showed a trace of impatience now — "I haven't got all night."

Tony looked around the room again. Over the toilet, the only window was covered with translucent paper in a stained-glass design. It looked painted shut. Beyond the bathroom door was the room with a ceiling hung with folds of material like a tent from the mirror over the oval bed. The soft material had moved gently with the breeze from the air conditioner, or was it only Tony's imagination? He shuddered, closing his eyes against the pink light.

"Tony," Bertoli said through the door. "You want the job or the cops? Make up your mind."

The anger in the voice roused Tony from his numbness. He stood up on the toilet seat and pushed experimentally at the window. The painted metal latch gave slightly. The space was small, but so was Tony.

"I'll give you five more minutes. But so help me, if you

screw up like this on a client, I'll bust your ass. You hear me?"

"Just a minute, Mr. B." Tony wrenched the window open, letting in a burst of hot damp air. His feet on the wainscoting, he shoved his shoulders through the tiny space.

With a final push, Tony wedged his hips through the window, urine trickling down one pant leg, and grabbed the fire escape in the darkness. He caught a glimpse of lights, and the black river in the distance.

Behind him, the door opened.

"You stupid prick! You wanna get killed?" Bertoli shouted behind him.

Tony jumped the gap to the next row house and grabbed onto the slate roof. Wet leaves slipped under his feet. Panting, he scrambled over the gutters and down the other side.

"Stop! Thief!" he heard Bertoli shout. "Stop him!"

Below, a light went on. A woman's silvery scream.

Tony grabbed the rusty metal of another fire escape and slid down. His feet touched wood. In the darkness, he knocked into plants, spilling dirt. Nearby, a woman screamed again. Dogs began to bark.

Breathing deep, Tony jumped feet first, off the deck into the branches of a tree. Sticks jabbed him, and he closed his eyes, slipping steadily down, hands bloodied from the bark. Below him lay the asphalt of a parking lot, the metal car roofs shining in the high-intensity crime lights.

His hands weakening, Tony jumped again toward the pavement. His coat grazed the metal dumpster, and he fell on hands and knees, pain shooting up from the skin torn off his hands. For a moment, he lay stunned, crouched on all fours on the asphalt. Then he scrambled up and ran bent over for the shadows.

9

The wolf had gone to his evening lay-up when he caught the scent of the big gray bitch, the same scent he had smelled his first night in the city.

Slowly, he nosed to the alleyway entrance, trying to fix the direction. The evening wind ruffled the hairs on his coat, sending his mane prickling up and down along the shoulder blades.

Whining, he edged out towards the street. Without the security of dog companions, he traveled furtively, corner to corner, the way he would have stalked strange territory in the wild.

The wind shifted, and he stood for a long time under a fire escape, drinking in the air and listening with his huge ears focused forward first in one direction, then another.

He heard the man-voice he associated with the bitch.

The voice called and shouted, conveying anger. Then it stilled. He heard the man's steps die away, and a door close. Far away, a chain rattled inside.

When the wolf turned into the wind again, the scent overwhelmed him. The bitch was full in heat, her smell cloyingly sweet and strong. Forcing himself to caution, the wolf padded along the scent through streets, into alleys, squeezing in gaps between sagging fences.

She stood tail down between two parked cars, nosing at an empty milk carton.

As the wolf moved upwind of her, she scented him and swung around. She began to whimper, backing up against a car. The wolf approached slowly, head low in appeasement, but the bitch was still nervous. Tucking her tail between her legs, she circled around a clump of asters and bared her teeth.

The wolf halted two car-lengths from her and squatted down on his belly, wagging his tail. He drew his lips from over his incisors, and whined invitingly.

The bitch stared at him in amazement. There had been no ritual in her matings with dogs. She barked at him in alarm.

Patiently, the wolf tried another tack. He sat up and cocked his head to one side for a moment, whining like a puppy. Then he began to dance slowly back and forth, still wagging his tail, with his head slightly lowered in submission.

The bitch hesitantly wagged her tail, but kept her back toward the wolf.

Gradually, the wolf circled in closer to her, prancing like a puppy with a stick in his mouth. The bitch's tail wagged upwards. Suddenly, the wolf darted close, sniffed her nose, and backed beyond her reach. She gave an excited little yelp.

Several times, the wolf advanced and retreated, until the bitch's tail wagged steadily. Slowly, the bitch moved sideways in a little dance of her own. The two circled around and around the parking lot behind the brick buildings, in and out of the halo of the anti-crime light, snuffling and licking. Beyond the parking lot wall, traffic roared in a steady hum on Storrow Drive, and the smell of the Charles River bank blew over them with the breeze.

Tail completely up, the bitch moved her hindquarters in slow, erotic motions. The wolf mounted her, side first, and licked her with the quick tongue-flicks he used to greet his mate and Vinnie.

The wolf mounted her again from the rear; the two rocked sideways for a while. Then, the wolf dismounted, and lay down facing away from her. They lay quietly, joined tail to tail, panting under the ragweed plumes.

They were content. The last crickets sang around them, and beyond the wall, the CITGO sign's red pyramid blinked on and off, on and off, over the black water.

In the dim light of the imitation gas lamps, the wolf trotted alone again. He was always hungry now. Although he fed often, scavenged trash could never equal what Vinnie had always fed him.

Under a bench he sniffed eagerly at the meat-smell of a motionless man wrapped in a long torn overcoat. But life still pulsed through the body. The wolf backed off.

The Common was quiet. Clouds hung over the stars, but the streetlamps and the neon of the theaters and fast-food stores that bordered the Tremont Street edge gave more than enough light for a wolf. Under the trees heavy with dampness, vague human shapes huddled on benches. A small dog nosed in a pile of newspapers like a jackal scavenging a battlefield. Tall grass and fast-food wrappers spread out under the streetlamps, glowing with water droplets.

Avoiding the paved paths, the wolf leaped the ditch into the unfenced cemetery across from the tennis courts, padding through the tall grass and rotting leaves. The wolf lifted one leg and urinated against a headstone, throwing his scent mark high.

When he had finished, he caught the smell of the boy. The wolf paused, reading him. There was no fear or aggression in the sweat-smell, but the body movements clearly showed pain.

Tony stared back at the yellow eyes that glowed under the streetlamp.

Last spring, a bearded man in jeans had spoken in the auditorium after lunch. First he showed a film about wolves trying to kill a moose in the snow. Tony had liked that, especially the scene when the moose lowered his head and charged the pack, scattering his pursuers.

Frankie and Patrick Noonan had begun throwing spitballs, but Tony watched the man lead out a huge German shepherd–colored dog, its head lowered. The bearded man had asked them all to howl, and the kids had happily wailed and yodeled until the walls rang. But the wolf merely sat on its haunches and stared at them as if they, not he, were the wild animals. Tony, feeling foolish, had not howled.

"You're a wolf," Tony said aloud, his voice coming out harsh and choked. He realized then that he had been crying.

The white wolf stepped closer and stood expectantly before him. The broad feet made no sound on the leaves. Slowly, the great tail swung from side to side.

Tony felt in the pockets of his blazer. In the right-hand side was the crushed remains of an Italian sub, wrapped in wax paper.

"You hungry?" he asked, almost expecting the animal to answer him, like a shape-changing magician in a story. Nothing would surprise him now.

Tony knelt in the wet leaves and held the sandwich out on his palm with the fingers flat — the way Ma had shown him how to feed a police horse. He held his breath.

The wolf stepped daintily forward and took it, dropping it in the leaves and chewing with the side of his jaw like a cat. Suddenly, he turned his head to one side and seized Tony's forearm between his teeth. Tony felt the razor incisors piercing the cloth. Hot saliva soaked his skin.

Tony's stomach turned, but he kept his body still. The teeth gripped him firmly, but did not penetrate the skin. Then, gently, the wolf released him and wagged his tail.

Tony breathed again.

The wolf whimpered, as if he expected Tony to reciprocate the gesture.

Slowly, Tony reached out and touched the fur around the wolf's neck. The outer guard hairs were bristly, but the undercoat felt soft and warm. The wolf made no move to retreat. His breath fell on Tony's face — hot and rank, but oddly comforting.

Carefully, Tony began to scratch the wolf around the ears and neck, the way he used to scratch the dogs. The fur was warm on his cold fingers. The wolf half-closed his eyes with pleasure.

"You like that?" Tony whispered. His voice came more easily now. The tears had dried on his face, and he put up one hand to scratch himself where the salt itched.

In an instant, the wolf was gone into the shadows. He was alone again.

Tony stood up slowly, aching as if he had been beaten. In the darkness, the tombstones were gray slabs, but Tony remembered the words from his favorite. In the quiet, he said them aloud. "Stop here my friend as you pass by. As you are now so once was I. As I am now so must you be. Prepare for death and follow me."

Tony brushed dead leaves from his knees, shook his hair back, and started down to the path to Tremont Street, heading south.

10

As the sky grayed, a mockingbird began to sing. Rounding the corner, Tony saw the windows of the house still dark. During the long walk through South Boston and Dorchester, he had picked in his mind the best hiding place — the lilac bushes close to the end of the driveway. The cover of the tall weeds where the lawnmower couldn't reach would hide him, and the branches overhead give cover from the morning sun.

Tony slapped a mosquito, and settled onto the wet grass to wait. It was a strange feeling to be spying on his own home, not as a game anymore.

From his shelter, Tony heard the small changes of the morning: the songbirds, a scattering of firecracker bursts, the rasp of katydids, the increasing traffic, the whirr of bikes and roller skates. First Tony's older brother left, shirtless and disheveled, for his paper route. Then Tracy with her paper bag full of doll clothes, and Erin with a bathing suit rolled in a white bath towel to the bus stop to wait for the settlement house daycamp van.

The kids who hung out at the tennis courts swaggered by, bare-chested, sunburned, their white-blond heads shaved in whiffles, and their boom boxes turned up full. The white Hoodsie ice-cream truck rattled down the street, playing its same music-box nursery rhymes over and over.

Tony's hunger was gone now, replaced by a terrible

thirst. But the Old Man was still there, one wheel of his car rolled onto Ma's marigold bed. Tony had helped her plant those marigolds in spring, with seeds she had saved from the dead flowers of the year before. In May, he had watered the new plants with the garden hose, careful to give them only a fine and gentle spray. Later, they had thinned them, feeling under the new green leaves for weak, spindly stems and pulling them out. Only the strongest should live.

Tony shut his eyes in the heat and thought of the cool spray from the hose arching over the plants. A rainbow glittered in the water droplets, and white cabbage butterflies opened and closed themselves on the yellow flowers. Cool water ran over his nose and down his face, and clouds of butterflies settled around him, now yellow and orange as the marigolds.

When Tony woke, the Old Man's car was backing out, so close to him the exhaust filled his throat. He didn't cough. Tony counted slowly to one hundred. Then he stood up, stiff and sore, rubbed his raw hands on the grass, and walked to the back door.

"Oh my God, what happened to you?" Ma said.

Tony shrugged. "I'm okay."

They stood staring, like two strangers. Tony noticed, for the first time, how small she was. Their eyes were no longer level. He hadn't noticed before how thin her hands were, the blue veins showing at the wrists. Her eyes were greenish flecked with brown, like Tracy's.

"You hungry?" she asked.

Tony nodded. The kitchen was unchanged: the same

pile of letters at the end of the dinette set, school artwork held to the refrigerator door with magnets in the shape of apples and ears of corn. The dogs pattered in as usual to sniff him, then retreated to the cooler hall. But to Tony, lifetimes had passed.

Ma turned in the middle of salting the eggs. "I better call the police, Tony, and cancel the A.P.B. Otherwise they'll be looking for you."

Tony shook his head.

Ma slid the eggs onto a plate and set them before him, and watched him eat.

"You're growing, Tony. I can tell. You're going to be a big man."

Tony swallowed a mouthful and drank half the glass of milk. "Don't call, Ma. I ain't staying."

"I can talk to your father. It'll be okay. You know he don't mean it half the time. You know that."

Tony scraped the last of the eggs, went to the refrigerator, and pulled out the bread. His drawing was still taped to the door.

"Tony, you know you aren't that kind of kid. You know that," Ma said.

Tony stuffed a slice of bread into his mouth. "I can't stay, Ma."

Ma watched him eat two more slices and pour himself another glass of milk.

"I got to take care of a sick cat before I go to work," Ma said. "Could you give me a hand?"

"Tammy get hurt?" he asked.

"No," Ma smiled. "It's a stray. Tracy found him up to

the park with an infected leg. I got him down in the basement."

"He don't know about it?"

"He'd kill me," Ma laughed. "Thank God, this one's quiet. God, some of them sound somebody's torturing them just because you got the door shut! The vet charged me fifty bucks for the operation and the pills."

"Remember the five baby squirrels this spring?" Tony asked.

"How could I forget? You kids were so crazy about them the first few days, but after they got their teeth you didn't want to have nothing to do with them."

Ma unlatched the cellar door at the end of the hall. Tony followed her down the wooden stairs. The old house had no real basement, but a dark, humid cave smelling of cat and floored with powdery gray dirt. The walls were rough granite boulders, like a dungeon in a sword and sorcery story. From the beams overhead dangled a single unshielded light bulb on a chain.

The cat lay on an old army blanket next to the furnace. A rangy yellow-striped tom, scarred on the face. It rose and stretched, arching its back as they came close.

"I ought to have my head examined." Ma knelt on the edge of the blanket. "Fifty bucks for this guy, and he isn't even my cat."

The cat butted its head against her thigh, purring.

"You hold him down while I clean the shunt. Then we'll give him the antibiotic," Ma said.

Tony grasped the cat's legs and forced it down onto

its side. It struggled briefly, then submitted, mewling like a tiny kitten.

Gently Ma swabbed the shaved space on one leg with rubbing alcohol and wiped off the plastic tubing protruding just below the knee joint. The cat quivered.

"It's all right, honey. Mommy won't hurt you," she murmured softly. "Silly cat, Mommy won't hurt you, Mommy loves you."

Tony gripped the cat's legs tightly. For no reason, he felt his throat constrict and his eyes begin to fill. Ma's shoulder touched him. He longed to be that cat, to lie down on the blanket and feel her cool hands comforting him, her voice murmuring to him. The thought came to him that he should hug her like a little child, the way her real children touched her, and lay his head against her thin shoulder.

Trembling, Tony turned his face away. Ma never hugged and kissed the older foster boys. Would she think he meant something dirty?

"I said, would you turn him over?" Ma said. "What's the matter, Tony? Are you sick?"

Tony's heart thumped against his chest.

"No, I'm okay."

"Tony, where'd you get those clothes?" Ma asked.

"Around."

"Please don't go, Tony. Please," Ma said.

"I have to."

Ma backed the tomcat between her legs, her feet folded under her Japanese fashion, and gripped the animal with her knees. Bending the head back with one hand, she dropped open the cat's jaw and squirted pink fluid from an eyedropper. Tony had never noticed how long a cat's incisors were, but Ma did not seem afraid. The cat writhed noiselessly, but did not escape. With one hand, Ma held the mouth shut and massaged its throat until it swallowed. With a bound, it leaped off the blanket, stalked into a corner, and began to wash.

"That'll teach you to get in fights," Ma said in the direction of the cat. How many animals had she nursed like that? Tony wondered. There always seemed to be something small and wounded in a cardboard box on the porch, something the neighborhood kids brought her.

Ma stood up, pulled the string on the light, and climbed the old wooden stairs.

"I'm going now," Tony said.

"No, wait. Take this," Ma went to the hall stand and pulled out her purse.

Tony shook his head.

"Look, you're entitled to it. It's really your money. It's not fair for me to get the welfare money when you don't live here."

Tony shrugged. "You keep it. I can make out."

Through the glass in the front door, Tony saw the two police cars draw up to the curb. The Old Man's car pulled up beside one, double parking. Ma stared, frozen, at the door.

"I didn't call, Tony. You know I didn't," she said.

"He must have seen me. The prick." Tony ran through the kitchen, out the back door past the trash cans.

Inside, the dogs began to bark.

From the corner of his eyes, Tony saw the cop in a short-sleeved shirt vault over the low white wooden fence and land in Ma's strawberry bed. He stopped for a moment to warn the man not to hurt the plants, but then remembered.

His heart pounding, every detail suddenly seemed clear to Tony.

At the end of the narrow yard stood a high wooden stockade fence where Ma's tomato vines were tied to the palings with string, the fuzzy stalks curling around hard green fruit the size of gumballs. The ground was soft where Ma dug every few days to loosen the soil. There was no way to climb the fence without breaking the fragile stems.

To the left, in Mrs. Termini's yard a tall black cop loped past the lilac bushes.

To the right, the white cop ran lightly toward him. As he ran, his hat flew off and sailed past Tracy's wading pool.

Tony stood still. There was no place but the fence to escape. I am not afraid, he said inside.

"Okay, let's go," the white cop said, panting a little from the run.

The other cop produced a pair of cuffs and unsnapped them.

Tony crossed his hands behind his back, the wrists together.

The white cop smiled and shook his head. "No, you empty your pockets first," he said.

Ma stood next to them, her face seeming more lined in the glare of the sun. In the background, the summer noises — lawn sprinklers, the whirr of bikes, cicadas — went on as if nothing had happened. Tony heard his older brother coming back from his paper route, kicking the bike's stand upright in the gravel driveway.

The matted grass, the old bikes, and the dirty swimming pool seemed infinitely precious now.

Tony pulled out a brown wallet with last month's Medicaid card, a house key, his MBTA student pass, some gum wrappers, and a Flair pen, and handed them to Ma, then crossed his wrists again. The cop gently patted him down. The cuffs snapped on with a small click, dangling loosely over his thin wrists.

Ma said nothing.

As they passed the front porch, Tony was glad his brother was now inside. The drone of the morning cartoons sounded through the open parlor windows.

Tony sat on the hot plastic as the black cop slammed the door without an inside handle. Tony looked straight ahead, until they were long past his own neighborhood.

11

"White German shepherd with black tips on the fur. It makes him look sort of gray," Vinnie Boudreau said to the girl at the Animal Protection League.

"Funny, I never saw a gray shepherd," she said, writing on a Xerox form.

"Well, he has some husky blood, I think. I mean, he's not one of your purebreds or anything." Vinnie coughed, shifting in his chair.

"Yeah. I think this whole purebred thing is a ripoff anyway." She brushed long hair back from her shoulders. "They want you to shell out several hundred bucks for essentially the same animal you could get here for ten. Weight?"

"Oh, about a hundred twenty-five pounds."

She whistled softly. "He *is* big. We don't get too many dogs that size, except maybe your Great Danes. Eats a lot, huh?"

"Yeah. He eats enough." Vinnie shifted his position on the hard chair and glanced around. The office was small and crowded. Books and pamphlets were piled on the floor between three rickety desks. Behind the girl on the wall was taped a poster showing a kitten and a puppy leaning on each other, their eyes wide, and printed behind them "THEIR ONLY CRIME IS BEING ALIVE!"

"Okay, that number is in Maine. But you lost him here."

"That's right." Vinnie hunched his shoulders.

The girl slipped the paper in a file jacket on her desk and stood up. Vinnie sighed, relieved that the questions were over. Under her lab coat, she wore one of the long Indian skirts that Vinnie had seen on the summer people. "I'm pretty sure your dog isn't here now, but you'd better have a look just in case."

Vinnie followed her through a fire door and down metal steps to the first floor. Even through the heavy doors, the barking and wailing of the animals filled the green cinderblock corridor. It smelled to Vinnie more like a hospital than a zoo — a dead disinfectant smell that would terrify any dog. Or wolf.

Inside the kennel, the noise was too loud for normal speech. The girl motioned at the cages: three tiers high, steel, with bolted doors and newspapers on each floor. Some dogs barked crazily and bit and clawed at the bars — the newcomers, Vinnie supposed. Others lay in heaps, not even bothering to look up as they entered.

The wolf was not there.

"Is that all?" Vinnie shouted.

She nodded her head. "Except the dead ones," she shouted over the barking.

"Could I see them too? Just to check?"

She started to shake her head, then nodded assent. Vinnie didn't look the type who would be freaked out by a few dead dogs.

Vinnie followed her through another hospital corridor. They passed a man in a white lab coat pushing a wheeled cage full of Labrador puppies, and opened a door marked ABSOLUTELY NO ADMITTANCE! In the center of the windowless room stood a large stainless-steel drum fitted with pipes and pressure gauges.

The girl unlatched the door of a walk-in refrigerator and motioned Vinnie to follow. Inside, the floor was covered with dead dogs and cats, wet with urine. But the wolf was not there.

As he turned back, the man in the lab coat fitted the wheeled cage into a slot on the side of one steel drum and opened the door. A window like an oven's showed the animals inside clawing frantically at the slippery walls. The man in the lab coat turned the wheel.

"There's no pain," the girl told Vinnie. "It's like what happens to divers who go too deep. They call it the rapture of the deep."

The Labrador puppies quivered for a moment, then collapsed in a huddle over each other. Vinnie could see no rapture.

Slowly, the man in the lab coat began to lay the puppies on the refrigerator floor with a shovel. "That's what I hate about this job," she said. "We're supposed to be protecting animals, but this place is a doggie Dachau. 'Oh, Miss, I'm sure you'll find them all *good homes,*'" she said bitterly.

She turned at the front door and shook Vinnie's hand. "Look, I'll keep an eye out for your shepherd, okay? We have a lot of calls for big dogs, so he wouldn't get put down anyway.

"Hey, I'm really sorry," she added.

Vinnie shrugged, opening the door into the hot air of the street.

12

The house stood near the top of a long hill, set back from the street behind a yard divided by stakes and pieces of white string into garden plots thick with dusty vines and ragweed.

Nearly half the clapboards — from the cupola to the Ionic columns of the porte cochere — were painted bright blue. The rest of the vast house had weathered gray like an old barn. At one corner, the iron skeleton of what had once been the conservatory jutted against an elm tree, the plastic sheeting that had replaced the glass shredded by the wind. As the wind blew, the elm tree creaked against the house, with a sound like wild geese calling. In the weeks Tony had spent in the halfway house in Brockton, summer had gone.

Tony's social worker drew the car up to the curb and cut the engine. "Lock it, will you?" she said.

Tony clicked down the lock on the Honda door, and shut it. Ms. Hayes was younger than most of them, but he would have known she was a worker or a teacher right away; the wire-rimmed glasses, the loose shirt, and the knapsack full of papers marked her. No girl from Tony's neighborhood would wear such ugly thick-soled shoes.

"Okay, Tony, this is it."

Tony followed her up the bare wooden steps. Over the mailbox, someone had hand-lettered *PROJECT TURN-ABOUT*. Inside, the wallpaper had been stripped, and all along the hall the walls were punctuated with cracks and spots plastered over with white spackling compound. Tony ran his hand over the grainy wall and the smooth plaster.

"How's the rehab work coming?" Ms. Hayes asked a tall man with bushy brown hair.

"You mean the building or the kids?" He smiled.

"Both," Hayes laughed. "This is Tony DiNatale. Joe Lucas, one of the housefathers."

"Where's the housemother?" Tony asked.

"There isn't one. I'm divorced," Lucas said. "But I'm open to suggestions."

"You want to do the papers, Joe?" Hayes asked.

Tony followed them into the kitchen and stood warily near the door, ready to leave if they wanted to talk about him. Lucas set a blackened tea kettle onto an old white enamel range, and turned on the gas.

Inside, the house did not seem as bad as it had looked at first. The linoleum was cracked, but a new dishwasher stood next to the sink. The room was warm, and smelled of coffee grounds and onions. Along the windowsill, a fat tabby cat lay stretched out, her eyes half-closed.

Scotch-taped over the counter was a blue poster of a huge gray bear with the lettering "Support the Right to Arm Bears!" Tony could find no clue to what the other kids were like. I am not afraid, he said in his mind. I am strong. I am not afraid.

"You want to check out your room, Tony?" Lucas asked.

Tony picked up the plastic trash bag that contained his

things and followed Lucas up the front staircase. Upstairs, the rooms were sunny, the wallpaper new. Only the pay phone at the end of the hall, with numbers and names scrawled on the wall around it, gave any sign that this was not a family home.

The room had two beds, one rumpled and the other neatly made, two identical dressers — one bare and the other cluttered with gum wrappers, old pictures, a baseball glove, and a tape recorder.

"Your roommate is Jerry," Lucas said. "He's from East Boston. About your size. And he doesn't snore."

"I don't either," Tony said.

"I don't expect perfection, but I don't want to come in here and find a lot of crap all over the floor, okay? The dirty laundry goes in here." Lucas flipped open a wicker basket. "Not under the bed or back in the drawers, or all over the closet floor, okay?"

Tony opened the bag and dumped the contents on the bed.

"You read those books, Tony?" Lucas asked.

"Yeah." Tony paused, wondering whether to unwrap his drawings and the paper bag with his colored pencils. He had put them in the bottom, sealed in layers of plastic bags with rubber bands, the way other kids hid their stash.

"You like to read?" Lucas asked, sitting on the messed-up bed. The cat walked in and rubbed itself against Lucas's long legs.

"Sometimes," he admitted.

"My favorite book when I was a kid was *Twenty*

Thousand Leagues Under the Sea," Lucas said. "You ever read that?"

"Yeah. I saw the movie on TV too." Tony thought of one of the movies he made in his mind at night: the gleaming black submarine half-submerged in tropical water, the wake casting white lights of phosphorescence, gliding silently past a deserted island, on the way to a terrible revenge on old enemies. "I thought the book was better."

"Yeah. I liked the book better too. That way you could imagine it the way you wanted. When I was a kid, we used to go on car trips, and I'd write myself into the story. Naturally, I always got a good part. You ever do that?" Lucas asked.

Tony shrugged and shook his head.

He sat down on the edge of his bed and began to sort out his socks and undershorts.

"I'll see if I can get you a bookcase," Lucas said. "There's a lot of old furniture around here."

Tony shook his head. "No, it's okay."

"Yeah, maybe you're right. The others might give you a hard time about it," Lucas said.

Slowly, Tony unwrapped the rubber bands and plastic from his drawings, and handed the roll wordlessly to Lucas.

Stretching them between his long fingers, Lucas studied each one. "I like the detail on the castle," he said after a while. "You ever had any training?"

"Ma — I mean one of my foster mothers — used to show me a couple of things."

"So this is your secret vice, huh?" Lucas asked.

"Yeah."

"Is that a wolf or a dog? The one in the graveyard?"

"A wolf. I saw him in the graveyard on the Common, you know, near the tennis courts? I fed him there a couple of times when I was on the street."

Lucas said nothing, but the small changes in his face showed Tony he did not believe him.

"I ain't shittin' you," Tony said. "He was white. This big," he held his hands off the floor.

"When was this?"

"About a month ago. Before I got busted."

Lucas handed Tony back the papers, and lifted the cat onto his lap. "You draw real well, Tony. I think you have a lot of talent. You should use it."

"I ain't goin' back to no school. Ain't no way," Tony said.

"You don't have any choice, Tony," Lucas answered. "It's the law. I can't keep you here unless you go to school. You already missed six weeks."

"Piss on the law," Tony said.

"All the boys here go to school," Lucas said.

"I want to be emancipated," Tony said slowly.

Under the bushy hair, Lucas's face drew into a smile. "Where'd you hear about that?"

"Around."

"Okay, I'll explain it. You could become an emancipated minor and eligible for welfare and your own apartment if you had a baby, which in your case is fairly unlikely. The other thing is that sometimes kids get kicked out of the foster care system because they're almost eighteen anyway, and they couldn't get a placement in time."

"I heard you could get out sooner."

"You hear a lot of stuff like that on the street. Look, if you don't believe me, I can show you the regs. I have a copy downstairs."

"No, it's okay, I believe you." Tony sat down on the bed next to the pile of undershirts.

Lucas stroked the cat gently along the ridge of its spine. Tony watched. Most of the families he knew had dogs, but he had never seen a grown man caress a cat before.

"I have a friend who's an artist. I think he'd be interested in your stuff. Maybe show you a few things. You want to think about it?"

"Yeah. Maybe I'll think about it," Tony said.

Downstairs, feet sounded on the wooden porch.

"Come on. I'll introduce you," Lucas said.

"No, wait!" Tony stuffed the drawings into a bag and crammed them in the back of a bureau drawer, his hands suddenly cold and clumsy.

Lucas waited until he was finished, and then walked with him downstairs.

In the half-darkness, Tony lay awake, watching Jerry's cigarette glow at the window. He could not sleep, though every muscle in his body felt strained with fatigue. His mind raced, like a car stuck in neutral. It had been the same in the house where he had waited for a placement.

Sometimes he would sleep all afternoon and through the night, then the next night lie wakeful, taut and jumpy as the kids who did pills.

Jerry sat at the window, his thin shoulders outlined by the streetlight, putting the cigarette to his lips.

Tony rolled over, turned the pillow over to the cool side against his cheek, and allowed himself to think about Ma.

I am not afraid. I am strong, Tony told himself. Ma bent over, the naked light bulb casting glints in her pale brown hair, and washed the cat's wound with the cotton ball soaked in alcohol. Then she drew Tony toward her and laid his head against her shoulder in the hollow of her collarbone, and stroked his hair as she had stroked the cat. Tony reached out to hug her the way Tracy did.

Tony sat bolt upright, his face hot, his heart racing.

"Nightmare?" Jerry asked in the darkness.

"Yeah," Tony whispered.

"Yeah, they're a bitch. I get 'em too. It's the movies. You seen the one where they cut the guy up with the buzz saw?"

"No, not that one."

"You didn't miss nothin', man. Hey, you wanna cigarette?"

"Okay, I pay you back tomorrow."

"Hey, don't worry about it. This one's onna house. I'm leavin' next week."

Taking a deep breath, Tony rolled out of bed.

"You got another placement?" Tony asked.

"No. I'm goin' home. Live with my brother. He owns a shoe store in Revere."

"No shit?" Tony said admiringly. "He got his own kids too?"

"Yeah. One baby. They got a real nice place in Malden. New Oldsmobile."

"You're lucky." Tony sat on the wide ledge beside him.

"Yeah, I'm lucky."

Tony flicked the match expertly between his thumb and forefinger. In the flare of the match, Tony saw Jerry's face was twisted with anger. Tony dragged deeply on the cigarette.

"I'm so lucky I'm gonna screw up like I did last time. The bitch," Jerry whispered.

Tony said nothing, waiting.

"You wanna hear a great story?" Jerry asked.

"Sure."

"I open the bathroom door, and there is my sister-in-law bare-ass bending over the bathtub. I mean, how am I supposed to know the broad takes a *bath* at three o'clock in the *afternoon?* And don't even lock the *door?* How am I supposed to *know* that?"

"So what happened?" Tony flicked the ash onto the floor.

"So you'd think I was Jack the Raper or something, and all I wanna do is take a piss! So she slams the door and locks it and starts screaming out the bathroom window, and the next thing you know the cops are here! 'Oh Frankie, I just don't feel *safe* the way he looks at me,'"

Jerry mimicked falsetto. " 'Oh Frankie, I don't think it's safe him here with the *baby*.'

"I mean, what does she think I'm gonna do to a baby? Eat it?" Jerry ground his cigarette against the windowsill. "Stupid broad," he murmured.

"So how come you goin' back?" Tony asked.

"She's gonna give me another *chance*," Jerry said. "Ain't that sweet? Another chance. She's gonna give her own brother-in-law another chance."

"Why don't you say the hell with them?" Tony asked.

"Cause it's blood. They're my family. They all I got. You got a real family?" Jerry asked.

"No. Not that I know of."

"That's too bad. Really," Jerry said.

"Yeah. I know." Tony leaned back against the wooden windowframe and stared at the window. The vapor lights shone yellow, illuminating the block around the variety store down the street with a false dawn. From the look of the small patch of sky beyond the towers of St. Buadan's, it would be truly morning soon.

13

With the shorter days of fall, the wolf's range began to change in small, inexorable ways. The locusts now were dead, their grubs burrowing in for their long life under the roots. The sumac and poison ivy reddened on fences, then the Virginia creeper changed, and at last the stressed maples, the honey locusts, and the elms. Willows in the Public Garden dropped dry yellow leaves into the pond mud. Aster flowers starred the weeds.

Even on sunny days, the earth was damp and rich with old smells.

Beneath the guard hairs, the wolf's undercoat began to grow in thickly, enlarging him even as his fat reserves were dwindling.

The wolf and the shepherd were scavenging on the Common when a Doberman with a red leather collar approached them. The wolf scented him first, and wheeled around to observe. The Doberman lowered his forequarters slightly and growled.

The wolf watched him, puzzled. The Doberman had no tail, and his ears had been surgically frozen in the pricked-up position. Like a deaf mute with no hands, he couldn't signal his intentions. But the wolf smelled no fear from the anal glands. The shepherd stepped back in deference to his leader, and the wolf and Doberman circled silently, searching out each other's weaknesses.

They closed briefly, jaws seeking a side grip on each

other's necks, then broke off. The shepherd stood still, whining. Then the wolf sprang at the Doberman. They wrestled for a moment, then suddenly the Doberman rolled on his back, knees drawn up like a puppy, and bared his belly to the wolf.

The wolf stood over the Doberman victorious for a moment, then broke into a run. The Doberman and shepherd followed. The wolf let them catch him, then the shepherd broke away with the other two in pursuit. They played tag until all three were exhausted, and lay with their shoulders touching in the sun on the asphalt path to rest.

After a while, the wolf rose and shook himself. Tails wagging, the three sniffed each other and followed the wolf toward his afternoon lay-up behind a dumpster. But the wolf hesitated below a fire escape, drinking in the wind. The other two sniffed also, but their sense of discrimination was not as finely honed as his.

The wolf began to track. Instead of trotting companionably beside him, the shepherd and Doberman followed Indian file behind with their noses lowered to the scent. After three blocks of stalking, the shepherd caught sight of the animal the scent belonged to: a silver gray longhaired female cat. She lay on a stone ledge below a ground-floor window, behind a wrought-iron fence, sleeping heavily for a cat. She was old, and the medicines her owner gave her for her various ailments had slowed her reflexes, as a lifetime in a small apartment had dulled her senses.

The wolf jumped the fence and rushed the cat. The cat leaped down into the flower beds and crouched with her back to the brick wall, her hair fluffed into a prickly mass. The wolf hesitated a moment, keeping his face out of reach of her claws, and lunged sideways.

The cat bolted between the fence into the alley, but the Doberman blocked her retreat. As she turned to claw him, the wolf seized the back of her neck and broke it with a jerk.

The wolf dragged the kill into an alley and fed while the others looked on. He would have permitted them to share his kill, but they hung back, sniffing and wagging tails with excitement. Food to them was mush from a can. The smell of live blood and flesh thrilled them, but it was not connected in their minds with eating.

When he had eaten the soft parts and most of the flesh, the wolf turned again to the other two, and all three circled tightly, licking muzzles and sniffing and half-mounting each other, feeling each other's warmth and strength. The dogs began to yip, and the wolf shut his eyes, cupped his lips over his teeth, and howled. Caught up in his emotions, the shepherd howled too, and the Doberman broke into long, harsh barking.

Abruptly, the pack howl was over. The three lay down together, heads on flanks, like a litter of puppies, and slept.

14 🔥🔥🔥

Lucas locked the heavy wooden door that faced Chestnut Street. "So what do you think of my old place?"

Tony looked down toward Charles Street, unimpressed. "No yard," he said, zipping his jacket.

"Some of these houses have walled gardens. This is a very high-class neighborhood, Tony," Lucas smiled.

"So?" Tony shrugged. "There's too many people. I wouldn't live here."

"Where would you want to live, if you could live anywhere?" Lucas asked.

"In the country. A real big place, you know? Big yard. Pool. And a bunch of big Dobermans so nobody'd rip off my stuff."

"The American dream," Lucas smiled.

In the soft evening light, the old brick row houses seemed gentler in their outlines, like stone steps that had worn from sharp rectangles into easy slopes. The bright geraniums and impatiens that had decorated the tiny front garden plots and window boxes in the summer were gone, and the brick sidewalks, scattered with dead leaves, black under the imitation gas lamps.

Tony carried his drawings and paints in a black plastic portfolio under one arm, no longer concealing them.

Lucas wore a Nikon around his neck on a woven strap.

"This is my last month here," Lucas said. "I don't make

enough for here now. I'll be in with you guys till I find another place."

"You used to have a better job?" Tony asked.

"No, not really. I never made much money. It was Barbara who made the money. My ex-wife. She works for a bank. I guess I was your basic kept man."

"If she had so much bread, why did you split?" Tony asked.

"It wasn't just one thing. I wanted kids, that was part of it. People here have really different ideas from the people you know, Tony. They don't have to worry about survival, so they get all bent out of shape about the details."

Tony shook his head uncomprehending. "If I had a lady with a lot of bread, I'd be real nice to her," he said. "She pretty?"

"I guess so. But when you live with somebody, that isn't too important after a while."

Lucas and Tony crossed Beacon Street into the Public Garden.

"Mister Lucas," Tony said softly. "It's him. Over by the lake."

"It's who?"

"The wolf. Remember I told you?" Tony stood still now, watching intently.

"Tony, there aren't —" he began.

The white shape detached itself from the shadow of a willow tree and drifted into the cover of a bush, like a leaf blowing in the wind. It moved like a wild animal.

"Oh Jesus," Lucas whispered. "You stay here, Tony."

"Is he really a wolf?" Tony asked.

"Don't move, Tony," Lucas said. "If you have to move, go forward or back, not sideways."

Gently, Lucas lifted the camera from his chest, ducked his head, and removed the strap. The shadow in the bushes was still. A couple walked by them, holding hands, and then a man swinging a long black umbrella. Two rats skittered across the grass and disappeared into a plastic bag.

"No, don't," Tony breathed at Lucas. "You promised you wouldn't tell. You promised."

"Be quiet," Lucas mouthed. The wolf stood still, not detecting danger from the camera. Tony watched him, his mouth dry with tension.

"You promised you'd leave me alone. You promised," Tony said aloud.

"Shut up, Tony. This is serious," Lucas hissed. He dropped to one knee, like a hunter.

The wolf still moved lightly down the path nosing at trash, oblivious to the man and the boy.

Lucas pressed the shutter, advanced the film, and pressed again.

Tony ran toward the bushes, waving his arms above his head, straight at the wolf. "Go! Run! They'll get you!" he screamed.

"Hey, Tony," Lucas yelled, still kneeling. "Hey Tony, cut that out."

"Run, wolf, run!" Tony shrieked.

The wolf bolted from the shadows, stared at Tony for a moment, then loped off towards Beacon Street.

Lucas pressed the shutter, advanced the film, and pressed again until the roll was finished. "Tony?" He looked up. "Hey Tony, where the hell are you?"

It was raining when Jerry opened the door. Tony stood on the porch, wet through to the skin, his plastic portfolio wedged under the front of his Barracuta jacket.

"Well, look who's here. Hey, Picasso, where you been?"

"Mr. Lucas still up?" Tony asked.

"I dunno. He's in his room. You want me to check?"

"He call the cops?" Tony peeled off his jacket and laid it on the floor. He began to shiver, teeth rattling.

"Nah. He talk big, but he never do that. He ain't got no balls," Jerry said.

Throwing from the shoulder, Tony hit Jerry to the side of the jaw. Jerry fell back against the heavy newel post. "You crazy or somethin'?" Jerry gasped.

Tony followed with a left to the stomach. From the stairs, Sean launched himself at Tony, pinning his arms back. Kevin followed, rolling him down.

"Leave me *alone!*" Tony shouted.

"Leave *you* alone? Asshole!" Jerry shouted. "You crazy, man!"

"Hey, it's the Man," Sean shouted.

"He's crazy!" Jerry winced, his face white against the scarred mahogany railings. "Man, I'n't do nothin', and he come at me!"

"Okay, everybody shut up." Lucas walked down the hall. Like the kids, he wore jockey shorts and a T-shirt. For an odd moment, he seemed to Tony like one of them, overgrown and awkward. "What's the story?" Lucas asked.

"Guy comes in here and he *hits* me. Shit, man, he's *crazy*."

Kendo came softly down the stairs and stood listening, his arms folded across his chest. He wore his white martial arts suit, too short, his bony ankles sticking out the bottoms.

"I thought you ran again, Tony," Lucas said.

"Leave me *alone*," Tony answered. "You can't leave *him* alone. You can't leave *me* alone. Why can't you leave me *alone?*"

"Leave who? What he talkin' about, man?" Kevin asked.

"The wolf! Why can't you leave him *alone?* Why?" Tony's eyes filled, but he fought it. "He's doin' okay."

"He's not doing okay, and neither are you. Okay, guys. Tony has been feeding a real live wolf. W-O-L-F. As in Little Red Riding Hood."

"Downtown," Kendo said. "He tole me. I believe him."

"Shit, man, you all crazy," Jerry rubbed his jaw. "What you been smokin'?"

"Believe it, Jerry, I got the pictures to prove it," Lucas said.

"What you gonna do?" Sean asked. "Shoot him?"

"No. I had some other ideas," Lucas said.

"Such as?" Kevin and Sean sat on the bottom step, their knees drawn up, alike, as if they were waiting to be told a story.

"First I have to find out if he's somebody's pet," Lucas

said. "You never know. Some fools will keep anything on a leash. Then they get sick of it and turn it loose. We had a woman with a cougar in the Back Bay a couple of years ago — he was real cute until he almost took her arm off."

"Why can't you leave him alone?" Tony said again.

"Cause the cops'll waste him," Kendo whispered.

"Yeah, Jesus, they'd love to kill him. Wow," Kevin said.

"Hey, we could keep him here. Tell Miz Hayes we got us a guard dog," Jerry giggled. "This is a dangerous neighborhood."

"Yeah, we making *sure* this is a dangerous neighborhood." Sean poked him.

"Hey yeah, he kill every dog onna street," Kevin laughed, poking back.

Tony stood up, still trembling in his wet clothes. "Up yours!" he shouted. "You think it's a goddamn joke! Well maybe I ain't laughing!" he sobbed.

Shaking his wet hair out of his face, Tony plunged up the long flight of stairs, stumbling and then recovering on the last step. The others listened as his feet ran down the hall to his room and the door slammed.

Usually, they would have laughed at him, but they did not. Instead, they sat in silence. Even the twins were still, their bony knees touching.

"You sure it's a real wolf? Like in the woods?" Jerry whispered.

"Yeah, I've seen them in Alaska," Lucas said.

"Downtown?"

"Yup. We saw him tonight. I'm pretty sure I got one or two clear pictures."

"Way out," Jerry murmured. "Wait till I tell my brother."

For a while, they were silent again, listening to the rain beat steadily on the gabled roof, and the elm tree moaning against the iron framework of the conservatory. The night sounds of late summer were gone. For the first time since spring, it seemed cold in the old house.

15

The white shepherd was a large dog, his gait only slightly marred by a congenital hip deformity. His color too was wrong — white and pale yellow except for a black muzzle and ears that gave him the look of a rangy sheep. He had been given away to a commune a mile down the road instead of sold for the $500 the breeder hoped he would bring. Since he had come to live in the city, he wore a homemade collar with a silver Eye of Horus and a name tag under his neck with his name engraved in flowing Celtic script.

Despite his large size, the white shepherd was the pack's outcast. Time and again, he would challenge the wolf to fight, and the wolf would bare his incisors and back him away. The white shepherd would cringe and submit; then the other dogs would nip at his flanks until he fell behind.

For days, he would trail the pack at a distance, sniffing their scent markings, mouthing what was left of their kills, until he gathered his courage for a fresh assault. Though the others felt free to nip him if he got close, the wolf never touched him.

In the Public Garden, the pack laid up under the low branches of a yew tree. It was always cold, and the wind and gray rain came every day. Food was scarce on the Common and the Garden now that no one ate on the park benches, yet the wolf still searched there, attracted by the smell of rotting leaves and growing things lying dormant under the ground. The scents held strange feelings that the asphalt and stone never evoked in him.

The pond had been drained, and the empty swan boat docks rose above a bed of Styrofoam cups, papers, and dried leaves. The wolf watched the brown ducks as they poked along the edges, muttering to each other, flanked by pigeons fluffed up against the cold. In the rain, no one brought them bread.

The wolf began his stalk downwind of the pond. He worked in slowly, freezing every few steps, like a pointer, one paw raised slightly off the ground. About six feet from the bank, he rushed the ducks.

Birds exploded into the air, but the wolf was lucky. He tightened his grip on a mallard and shook it, snapping the neck the way a puppy kills.

Behind him dogs began to bay. Their sound covered the

noise of the approaching horse until the wolf felt its hoofbeats through the earth.

The wolf kept hold of his kill and ran lightly toward the lay-up, but the horse, goaded by the man, was faster.

"Get outa here! Git!" the policeman yelled. "You goddamn mutt!" he screamed, sawing on the reins.

The bay horse leaped between the wolf and the pack. The dogs began to jump and bark with excitement. Swiveling his head to ease the pain from the bit, the bay caught the wolf's fear scent full in his nostrils.

The wolf drew back on his haunches, and the horse flailed at him wildly with shod hooves.

The man dug his knees in, but the horse dislodged him. He slipped to one side, grabbed at nothingness, and fell on his hip onto the wet grass.

Freed of the weight, the bay reared back and struck at the wolf. One hoof hit at his rib cage, the other his forepaw.

The wolf dropped his kill and snapped at the bay's nose. Suddenly, the dogs were circling the bay like a deer, nipping and barking. The bay reared up again, his eyes white, and bounded off across the grass toward the spiked fence.

The wolf seized his prey and ran with it on three legs, the dogs streaming behind him.

"Hey, come back, Dante!" the man yelled, his yellow slicker open, and his pants soaked with mud. "Come back here, stupid!"

"Stupid horse!" he yelled. "Come back here." A city childhood of Saturday afternoon Westerns at The Strand had not prepared him for the nervous idiocy of real horses.

The bay screamed as if answering him, but careened back and forth along the fence, unable to see the open gate in his panic.

Brakes screeched along Arlington Street.

"Dante!" the cop shouted again, and the bay halted for a moment, long enough for the gate to register on his limited vision. He leaped through. Another squeak of brakes, and then silence.

"Ah Jeeesus, Jeesus," the man repeated mechanically. He began to limp toward the street, one hand on his hip.

The dogs were gone.

Lucas spread the black-and-white glossies out on the top of a long mahogany table for the four men and Tony to see. It was quiet in the paneled room that had once been the library. Light came dimly through an art nouveau stained-glass window onto a long expanse of pale oriental rug. Behind him hung a gilt-framed portrait of a gray Skye terrier named Tutu standing proudly on a windy beach. The actual Tutu stood about twenty feet away, preserved in a lifelike attitude, in a glass case in the Animal Protection League's lobby.

Lucas knew that the league's hospitals, the stables, a pet cemetery, two lobbyists against vivisection, a summer camp for pets, the dog pound, the staff, the executive director, the president, and his driver lived on the legacy of one lonely woman, and that dead dog.

Vinnie Boudreau fingered the clearest print and nodded to Lucas. "It's him. But he looks thin now."

Tony fidgeted in the big leather chair beside Lucas. He had seen rooms like this only in old movies. At the head of the table sat Kelton V. Chapin, the league president, looking as Tony imagined a senator or a Mafia don must look — tall, tanned, and immaculately gray in a dark suit. Tony examined the room carefully, pretending he was drawing. It seemed strange that all this splendor had to do with stray dogs.

Chapin spoke in a deep voice, like the man from the cardinal's office whom Tony had seen at summer camp on opening day. Why did he bring me? Tony wondered. "This is Captain Dan O'Meara of our Enforcement Division." A heavy man in a police uniform stood up. "Dr. Robert Eisler is senior biologist with Fish, Game, and Wildlife." A military-looking man with a white crewcut nodded. "And Vincent Boudreau, the owner of Wild Animal Park."

Vinnie was the kind of man Tony had known all his life. He could imagine him in a La-Z-Boy chair with a can of beer, watching *Charlie's Angels*. But he had raised the wolf.

The other men looked at Vinnie, as if expecting him to speak. He cleared his throat, and glanced nervously around. "I don't want to make no trouble. If you got to put him down, you put him down."

"Nobody's talking about putting him down," Lucas said.

There was silence. Tony could feel the tension between

the men. His legs ached to take him out of the chair and away, but he could not move.

Then O'Meara spoke. "All right, if that's the way you want it, I'll be the bad guy. You're going to have to call in a game warden and put him down."

"I thought this place was called the Animal *Protection* League," Lucas said.

"Let's stick to the facts," put in Chapin.

"Okay, let's *stick* to the facts. I called the Isle Royale wolf preserve, and they said they'd take him. It's an island, and there's no chance of escaping."

"All right then." O'Meara drummed the polished table with his fingers. "How do you get him in the shipping crate?"

"With a tranquilizer dart gun. I've seen it done," Lucas said.

O'Meara shook his head. "Shooting an animal in the woods and shooting an animal in a crowded city are two different things. The cartridge is a syringe this long," he said, holding his fingers apart three or four inches. "If that thing ricochets off a wall, you're in big trouble. Even if you hit the animal squarely, you could kill it anyway if the syringe perforated the pleural cavity or the abdominal wall.

"Plus your animal is pretty streetwise by now," he added. "My guess is you'd be lucky to get one clear shot before he takes off."

"He never hurt none of us," Vinnie said suddenly. "You can ask Marie."

"Of course I'm not an expert like you, but I've done a fair amount of reading. Isn't it true that there isn't *one* authenticated case of a wolf attacking a human being in North America?" Lucas asked, turning to Eisler.

Eisler gazed across at Lucas, then at Tony. "That's true. In the wild. This animal has been imprinted on man, which is another story."

"Why?" Lucas asked. "He's been raised like a dog. And God knows I've seen bigger dogs than that roaming the streets every day! I mean, what is the *danger* in waiting to take him alive?"

"All right," Eisler said. "I'll give you an example. Last summer two captive wolves mauled children's arms on two separate occasions in a private zoo in Michigan. One of the boys was about his age"; he nodded at Tony. "Probably the boys were teasing him, but the fact is, it *happened*. I'm not saying this wolf would do that. I'm saying you can't be sure he *wouldn't*. I'm saying you cannot totally predict the behavior of any wild predator. When it comes to human versus animal life, it isn't worth the risk."

Tony wriggled in the chair, pulling his arm away from where the leather had stuck uncomfortably to his skin. Couldn't Lucas see it was useless, that you always lost in the end?

"Isn't the eastern timber wolf listed as an endangered species?" Lucas asked.

"That doesn't make one individual unique. There are about eleven thousand wolves in the United States, so he's not in the same league with the whooping crane. Anyway, he isn't part of a breeding wild population."

"He *would* have been," Vinnie said. "Guy from the Interior Department in Washington said they had a plan to restock some of the parks in the East with wolves. I still got the letter."

"A noble idea." Eisler shook his head. "Mr. Boudreau, besides the political factors, which I'm sure you're aware of, there are sound ecological reasons why it wouldn't work. The niche in the New England ecosystem left open by the extermination of the wolf is already being filled by the eastern coyote. I'm not going to get into whether or not the eastern coyote is a new species or just coyotes that have found their way east, but the fact is they're much better adapted to life on the fringes of man than the wolf. The coyote doesn't need a pack structure to hunt like the wolf. He's smaller and more of an opportunistic feeder and doesn't need a lot to fulfill his protein requirements.

"Believe me, I know how you feel about your animal emotionally, Mr. Boudreau. I've known several people who kept wolves, and it was a much stronger bond than you get with a dog. But here in New England a wolf is an anachronism. His time is past, and you can't change that. You're only prolonging his suffering by letting him live like a stray dog." Eisler toyed with the photograph. In the dark print, the white wolf shone indistinctly, like a ghost.

"He doesn't look dangerous to me," Tony said, speaking for the first time. "I scratched his ears," he half-whispered. Lucas nodded vigorously.

"Young man, I don't like this situation any better than you do," Chapin interposed.

"But I fed him. He don't want to die," Tony said.

Chapin pulled back his shirt cuff and studied his watch.

"Look, I'll try it myself, okay?" Lucas said. "If I screw up, your ass is covered. Just tell me where to get a dart gun. Vinnie will help. You can shoot, right?"

Vinnie nodded.

"Now just a goddamn minute." Eisler pushed back his chair. "Before you go prowling around this town on your mission of mercy, let me tell you a few unpleasant facts. I've been in this business twenty-three years, and one thing I have learned is that *nobody* is neutral about large predators. Nobody."

"I worked for Greenpace," Lucas began.

"I don't care if you worked for Noah on the Ark! I'm going to tell you this, and then you can do what you damn well please, but you're going to listen to me for one more minute. I have been down this road too many times with the wolf and the coyote. Every time you get hearings on predator control or protecting a wild population, it's the same damn thing. Some people get up on their hind legs and holler and scream for you to eradicate every wolf in the country because they're killing stock, and they're all bloodthirsty murderers.

"Then the eco-freaks get up on *their* hind legs and yell just as loud that wolves are all noble savages, and they only kill sick animals, and wolves mate for life — which seems to impress the hell out of them maybe because they'll hop in the sack with any warm body themselves — and no wolf ever harmed a human being. Believe me, neither side is *ever* going to convince the other.

"Mr. Lucas, when the words gets out — and believe me, it will — that there's wolf loose around here you're going to tear this town wide open. And *you* are going to be responsible."

Lucas rubbed his hands through his bushy hair, standing it on end. "Okay, give me a week. He's been here since August, and nothing's happened. What's one week more?"

"In my book human beings come before animals." Eisler pulled his jacket off the back of his chair and walked toward the door.

"Wait a minute," Lucas asked. "Are you going to the media?"

"I would *love* to go to the media if I didn't think the panic would be worse than the situation you have now."

"Then you're not going to the press," Lucas said.

"That's right. You know I always thought maybe you eco-nuts were a little crazy, but I didn't used to think you were stupid too."

The double doors closed with a click behind him.

"Give me a week," Lucas turned to Chapin. "Then you do what you want."

Chapin shook his head.

"Okay, three days. Three days or I tell all the 'eco-freaks' on your board of directors you had an endangered wild animal shot because you were afraid of bad publicity."

Chapin smiled down at Tony. "And what do you think

about this, young man? You were very brave to feed a full-grown wolf."

Screw you, Tony wanted to say to him. But the level gray eyes and the smooth voice unnerved him. Like the priest from the cardinal's office.

"I dunno," Tony shrugged.

"Give me three days," Lucas said.

Chapin stood up. Automatically, Lucas, Vinnie, and Tony stood too. "I'll give you two days." Chapin reached out and shook Lucas's hand, then patted Tony's head. "Keep me informed."

"I will," Lucas answered.

The heavy door closed behind them. From the adjoining hospital wing, in the silence, came the wails and barking of the dogs, dulled to a distant mutter.

"Come on, Tony," Lucas said. "We don't have much time."

16

"If you get too cold, get back in the van and start the engine, okay?" Lucas asked. "You know how to turn on the heater?"

Tony nodded, and Lucas handed him the keys.

Lucas stood in the shadow of the van, keeping the dart gun close to his body while Vinnie climbed out.

"The game's afoot, Watson," Lucas whispered.

"My name's Boudreau," Vinnie corrected him softly. "Vinnie Boudreau."

Lucas paused for an instant. "Oh, yeah. Boudreau. Okay, why don't we start with the alleys behind Charles Street? There's always a lot of garbage there from the restaurants."

Tony followed, walking fast. Even in the thermal underwear Lucas had bought him, his legs were cold when he stood still. In the row houses, a few yellow squares of light still shone, but most of them were dark.

In the darkness, Tony remembered the first time he had killed something. He must have been less than six. The worker had re-placed him because the foster mother was pregnant, and the trailer park only allowed one child. So he must have been just under six. Yet he saw it again clearly.

They had been walking through an open field. Tony remembered the woman as very young, in blue jeans and an embroidered shirt, with long dirty-blond hair. It was almost dusk, and a wood thrush called in the trees across the open grass.

Tony saw the flash of white tail at the edge of the wood-line, and threw the stone he carried with all his force. Twenty or thirty feet away, the rabbit flopped to the ground, as if somebody had dropped it.

Tony was always throwing stones at things. But he had never hit anything alive before.

Tony ran to the edge of woods and found the grass wet with red. The rabbit was gone. He plunged into the bushes.

"No! Come back here! You'll get poison ivy!" Mama shouted.

"But I hurted him!" Tony yelled, his feet catching on vines. A blackberry branch whipped thorns across one hand.

"Come back here! You can't do nothin' for it!"

"He's gone!" Tony wailed. "I killed him!" Tony flailed at the bushes, scratching his hands and face.

"Get out of there!" Mama shouted. "You're a mess." She jerked him into the clearing. "*Look* at your sweater."

"I killed it," Tony began to cry.

A half-mile downwind, the wolf caught Vinnie's body scent mixed with the smell of fear. The wolf rose unsteadily, licked his side, and limped to the corner of a building where he could better catch the night wind. He paused with one foreleg off the ground and drank in the cold air again. This time it revealed the small man who had fed him, his scent tinged with anxiety, and another man he didn't know.

The wolf hesitated, choosing to follow his hunger and ignore his fear. He limped along the wall of the building, keeping away from the lights of the streetlamps and windows. The shaggy yellow bitch that had been following him lately got up and padded after him at a distance, and a stray part-Labrador brought up the rear. A block behind, the white shepherd trailed them, sniffing for a long time at every corner.

The wolf stalked the three figures hopefully until he came within sight of the dumpster. As Vinnie's smell flooded his nostrils, crowds of old sensations rose up in his mind: steaming dry dead-food from a bag, with hot water poured over it; the tearing buzz of the chain saw slicing through a cattle carcass. Dry snow under his paw pads, and the leash pulling away and the first run free over the open fields. The bitch wolf's rough tongue, and her warm body pressed against his flank.

The wolf's hindquarters wriggled with pleasure. Then he froze.

As the two men moved, he understood the fear scent. The sticks they tried to conceal by pressing them against their bodies meant nothing to the wolf. But the way they walked, so slowly, so carefully looking around, and the subtle chemistry of their smells told the wolf that the men had not come to feed him. They were hunters now too. They moved and smelled like hunters. They had come to kill.

The wolf pressed his body painfully to the sidewalk, keeping away from the light. Then he began, as the men's eyes turned away, to inch backwards.

Tony thought, just for a moment, he saw the wolf's ears pricking up above a trash bag. But when he looked again straight on, he saw only dead leaves. He walked slowly after Lucas.

As the wolf retreated, the dogs came forward and lay down beside him in the cold. The white shepherd, emboldened by the wolf's injury and fear, trotted up and lay down about six feet from them, his ears flat with anxiety.

Then the white shepherd noticed they were all watching and smelling the three humans intently. He raised his head and tested the air. But the acute sensitivity to the patterns of hunter and hunted that the wolf possessed had been bred out of the shepherd, and he saw only two nervous men with sticks and a boy.

The shepherd rose and faced the wolf, and to his amazement, the wolf stood uneasily and lowered his forequarters in submission. The shepherd raised his tail high and bared his incisors in a low whine. But this time, the wolf simply walked off, favoring his injured paw.

Puzzled, the other dogs whined. The yellow bitch started after the wolf, but he lunged at her, and she retreated.

Full of triumph, the shepherd raised his head and tested the breeze again. The men the wolf had been afraid of were still standing there. But the shepherd was not afraid. He gathered his body into a leap and burst into the alleyway.

Lucas saw only the flash of white come from behind the dumpster straight at him. He pressed the dart gun against his hip and fired blindly. The weapon made a tiny hiss and a hollow thud as it pierced through flesh. Then a human sounding shriek cut through the silence, sliced off as if somebody had cut the screamer's throat.

Tony hung back while the two men ran toward the white body.

"My God, it ain't him." Vinnie knelt and showed Lucas the animal's head in the flashlight beam. The brown eyes were open, the eyeballs rolled up toward the lids. The body moved convulsively, a froth of blood gathering at the black lips. Then a stench as the dog's body wastes oozed out the sphincter onto the asphalt. Lucas drew back.

"Are you sure?"

"Yeah, I'm sure." Vinnie hooked his fingers through the leather collar and fingered the Eye of Horus. "This here's somebody's dog.

Lucas knelt beside the animal and felt through the fur to the dog's thick chest. There was no heartbeat. Then he saw the glint of metal. The whole cartridge was embedded through the chest wall, the bottom sticking out like the handle of some exotic weapon. Instead of injecting the drug, the impact had driven the whole syringe into the animal's vital parts.

"What the hell is going on?" Tony heard a woman's voice behind him. "You shot that dog! Who the hell do you think you are?"

"We're from the dog control unit," Tony heard Lucas answer.

"Dog *control?* What kind of control is this, shooting dogs?" another voice asked.

Lucas strained to read the Celtic script on the dog's name tag. "We'll have to notify the owner," he said.

"You won't have to, honey," a woman answered him. Tony looked up to see a thin face framed with stringy hair. Then a bearded bald man was beside him staring down at the dog.

"Gandalf," the man said to the dog. "Gandalf. I don't *believe* this!" His eyes turned to Lucas. "You bastard, you killed my *dog!*"

"It was an accident," Lucas said slowly. "I'm sorry, but there's nothing you can do now."

"See, we thought he was the wolf—" Vinnie began, then stopped.

"The wolf? What wolf?" the woman asked.

The bearded man knelt on the pavement and cradled the dog's limp head in his lap, its tongue lolling out. "Oh God, I don't *believe* this. The pigs killed Gandalf," he sobbed. "I don't believe this. I don't *believe* this."

"It was an accident," Lucas repeated stupidly.

"Oh, yeah, sure it was an accident." The bearded man was weeping, tears coursed down his lined face. "Oh sure. Hey, you go around with a rifle and it was an *accident!* Oh sure! Hey you really expect me to *believe* that?" The bearded man rocked back and forth over the dog's body while he spoke.

"Please, mister," Vinnie began.

"Hey well, listen!" he shouted brokenly at Lucas. "Listen, asshole, because you're gonna pay for this, understand! Understand? You're gonna *pay!* You get the picture?" he screamed at Lucas. "You get the idea, pig? You get the *picture?*"

The man spat at Lucas's face, but Lucas said nothing. Absently, he wiped the spittle off his cheek.

"Hey, Al, come on, baby," the woman with stringy hair said gently.

"Hey no way, no way they gonna get away with this, you understand?" the bearded man shouted. "You *understand?* You understand I'm callin' all the papers, the TV, everybody. You understand I'm gonna get a lawyer and sue the hell outa you? You understand the whole city is gonna *know* about this?"

"Hey, shut up for a minute, Al. What's the thing about a wolf?"

"What wolf?" another voice asked. "Hey, is that a wolf?"

"Oh Gandalf," the bearded man moaned. "Oh Jesus God, I don't *believe* this. I don't *believe* this."

Unnoticed, Tony backed into the shadows.

Slowly, Tony turned down Brimmer Street past the garage, and crossed Beacon to the place near the bronze statue of the lady throwing something from a basket where the Project Turnabout van was parked. The third key fit the door, and he eased himself up onto the high seat, turned the ignition, and started the engine. At first, the air coming through the vents was cold, and his breath ghosted in the air, but gradually the interior warmed enough for Tony to take off his gloves.

In the stillness of the cab, Tony studied the diagram incised on the black knob of the gearshift lever, and practiced shifting in the air. First gear up, second down, then up and across the H to third, then down to fourth.

He had watched Lucas do it so often, his long legs depressing and releasing the clutch and brakes, swearing softly as he wove in and out of the traffic patterns or tried to wedge the van into a parking space. Tony stretched his right leg down, then his left, and found that, with a little effort, he could depress the clutch and stay balanced at the edge of the bucket seat.

A girl in a down parka and high boots passed quickly, looking over her shoulder. Tony waved at her, but her face was turned away. The lights in the restaurant, and then the pub across the street went out. It must have been far past midnight, Tony guessed, yet he was still not tired.

He looked up the long brick slope of Beacon Street; there was still no Lucas.

Tony stared down over the flat steering wheel. He had driven Ma's car once in New Hampshire, and the cars of older kids in the park, but in the van he felt perched too high up, jutting out into the street as if he might fall out the windshield any moment.

The back of the van stretched dark and indefinite behind him. Tony peered down at the blue Chevy parked in front, released the handbrake, slipped the van in gear, and checked the side mirror. The street was empty. Slowly, he pulled into Beacon Street with his pulse thrumming in his ears. He gave the accelerator a tiny tap, and steered stiffly around the corner to Arlington Street, down the level stretch past the intersection of Boylston, into Park Square.

The light was red, but no cars were close. Putting in the clutch again, Tony yanked the lever back to second with a grinding metal sound. From the high seat, Tony looked down on the tops of parked cars. The next lights were green, and Tony wriggled the lever across the H, pushed the clutch as far as it would go, and shoved it with a satisfying click into third, steering to the right, down the long stretch of Columbus Ave.

Tony hunched over the horizontal wheel jockey-fashion, straining to keep his toes touching the accelerator, his right hand on the gearshift lever, and his left steering the horizontal wheel. It was like the game of patting your head, rubbing your stomach, and reciting a tongue-twister at the same time.

The lights flashed by faster now. Sweating in the heat of the closed van, Tony put in the clutch again and jerked down to cross back to second, but instead the engine lurched whining into fourth. Tony felt wildly for the brake pedal, but stamped down on the accelerator instead.

A red neon sign — RIBS — flashed at Tony as the van skidded past a parked Lincoln. For a moment, two wheels in the air, the van seemed to be performing a stunt from a movie car-chase sequence. Then it righted itself and drifted into a concrete pole supporting a streetlight. The concrete crumbled with a gigantic chewing sound, spurting tangled wires. The right front window threaded into a spiderweb of cracks, then exploded inward so slowly that to Tony it seemed like the images he saw when he was very stoned.

The van stopped, engine still running. Tony stared at the blank alley wall before him. Someone had pasted up layers and layers of old political posters, and over them all the black spray-painted scrawl *Mr. Mojo Risin!*

Tony slid off the high seat and pulled open the door on the driver's side, jumping down. Glass crunched under his feet.

Although his pace was slow, favoring one front paw, the wolf did not look back at the crowd of humans and the dead white shepherd. The old range was now the territory of other predators — predators who hunted him — and the wolf knew this area that he had learned and scent-marked so well was now no longer safe. He trotted steadily, choosing the darkest streets and alleys, leaving the old range behind.

In the alley next to a boarded-up Puerto Rican grocery, he paused to examine the scent markings, and breathe in the wind off the harbor. In the damp night air, he smelled the time of year when snow would come.

17

There was only one cigarette left in the pack of Viceroys. Vinnie took it out, crushed the pack up in his fist, and threw the wad in the direction of the trash can. It missed. The chimpanzee bounded off the sofa and scuttled after it, hooting with excitement. Crouching, he turned the crumpled ball over and over in his long hands. When he realized that it was empty, he threw it at Vinnie's head.

Vinnie laughed. "Atta boy, Bimbo! Here, you can have my last one. Cause you're my friend."

Vinnie held the cigarette up enticingly.

Bimbo propelled himself on his feet and knuckles back to the sofa and clambered up beside him. He bared his teeth in a parody of a grin and clapped his wrinkled black hands.

Vinnie handed him the cigarette. The chimpanzee popped it eagerly into his mouth, sucking at it. With some difficulty, Vinnie managed to strike a match and light it. Bimbo took a long drag, fingering the cigarette like a man.

"You gonna be the first goddamn monkey to git lung cancer, you know that?" Vinnie asked.

Bimbo rolled his eyes and hooted again. It was Bimbo's former owner, an advertising copywriter who had kept him locked in a Manhattan studio apartment, who had taught Bimbo to smoke. Marie hated it, and Vinnie only let him do it secretly. Now she was over at her mother's, driven off by the TV people and their questions and their trucks and lights and snaking electrical cords, and the two of them could safely indulge their vices together.

Vinnie poured another three fingers of Canadian Club into a paper cup and handed it to the chimpanzee. Bimbo took a large swallow, rolling it around in his mouth, and spat it onto the floor, wrinkling his flat nose in disgust.

Vinnie threw back his head and laughed.

"You're a smart monkey, you know that? Smart monkey!" Vinnie leaned his head back onto the crocheted doily on the back of the sofa bed and poured another three fingers into his own glass. "Smart monkey," he murmured pensively. "I been shitfaced with a lot worse guys than you, you know that, Bimbo?"

Bimbo nodded, his dark eyes shining at Vinnie.

"You're a good boy, Bimbo. A good boy," Vinnie murmured. He closed his eyes, letting the warmth of the whiskey wash over him. The air in the mobile home was warm and heavy with smoke, like a barroom. He nodded, and let his thoughts drift him gently far away.

When he woke, the room was cold and gray with dawn, Bimbo curled in the middle of a rumpled army blanket in one corner. Cigarette smoke hung unmoving in the dead air.

Vinnie raised himself full upright, shook his head, and opened the mobile home door. For an instant, the cold stunned him, tingling his nostrils. Then he breathed deep, clearing his awareness.

The moon was gone, and, over the edge of the line of scrub pines, the sky was a pale winter pink. Venus, the morning star, hung bright between the branches of an oak.

From the nearby pen, the mother wolf, the unmated male, and the nearly full-grown pups began to howl. To Vinnie, it seemed as though her voice had changed to mourning now, like a woman in some savage tribe keening the dead. Her bitter wails poured hopelessly into the cold air over the frozen ground, punctuated by the thin soprano *yip yip yip* of her children. The sound seemed too big, too terrible for such a small, mean yard, and he covered his ears with his hands.

In the half-light, he saw the bitch wolf had started her daily pacing next to the wire. Three steps to the right, turn around, three steps to the left, turn around, three steps to the right, on and on. The pups were still young and full of curiosity, leaping to the wire mesh for every visitor, casting about for scents in the cold wind. But soon they would begin to pace, Vinnie knew. Soon they would spend their waking hours pacing, stopping only to eat or sleep — unseeing, unresponding.

All their lives they would pace that pen, three steps to the right, three steps to the left, three steps to the right, three steps to the left until death brought them freedom.

It came to Vinnie suddenly — the day he had first thought of the Animal Garden. A large framed piece of embroidery had hung on the wall behind the rocking chair with the folded afghan in Miss Gifford's house where Ma worked on Saturdays.

He could see the picture still in his mind. The colors had faded under the glass, but the details were still clear: two pink-cheeked children in long white nighties stood in the foreground surrounded by all kinds of animals. A lion with a mane of yellow knots and a lamb made of gray tufts stood in front, and, crowded behind them, a long-horned cow and a spotted horse, a beaver, a pale orange giraffe, and a brown bear with yellow eyes, and some he couldn't figure out. Perhaps they were made-up, like dragons and unicorns.

Over all the animals arched pale green willows, and the background was bright with birds. When he asked her about it, Ma had studied it, and said at first it might be the Garden of Eden, but she wasn't sure because the children were too little to be Adam and Eve, and had too many clothes on, though perhaps in the old days people were more modest and added in the nighties so as not to shock the children. Besides, there was no snake, and none of the trees bore apples.

So Vinnie called it just the Animal Garden. He had thought about it a lot when he was small. In the Animal Garden, no one was ever cold or ashamed, or punished for things they hadn't done. At night, before he went to sleep, he imagined he was the little boy in the long white nightie, smiling and feeling the lion's warm fur, and his cold moist nose gently touching his cheek like a house cat.

Years later, in Korea, on the long cold nights huddled against the other men between the walls of a roofless hut, his mind had called up again the vision of the Animal Garden, the feel of soft fur and gentle eyes. When he first heard about the park for sale, he had thought of renaming it the Animal Garden like his dream. But then, all the signs and the legal papers, and the old billboards up and down 1-A said Wild Animal Park, and it seemed a lot of trouble to change them. He would do it one day, once he really got the place fixed up.

Now in the dawn light, as he looked out at Wild Animal Park through the accusing eyes of the TV people, he saw what he had always seen, but tried to push back from his mind with hopes and love. The steel pens could never be an Animal Garden. Even if the animals could roam free without hurting the people, the visitors would torment them, give them trash to swallow, poke sticks at them, and laugh at their pain.

He saw that in trying to be kind, he had been cruel. That, for all his years of work, every day the reality of their lives, and his, became more degraded. Now nothingness was better.

Vinnie opened the camper door and took the .45 from the glove compartment. He walked to the wolf pen and watched the bitch wolf pacing, her toenails clicking softly on the rough concrete. The pups looked at him, sniffing him, rearing up on their hind legs like horses. The unmated male held himself back, head lowered, only his eyes moving.

Slowly, the way he had been taught, Vinnie placed himself with his legs planted far apart, his hands together, and his elbows stiff, sighting down the short barrel.

He stood for a long time while the crows called in the pine trees, watching the bitch wolf pace and the pups tussle. The unmated wolf's yellow eyes met his and stared, long and knowingly.

Vinnie let out his breath and dropped his hands. The .45 fell with a crunch into the dead catbriar vines.

From the pen, the wolves began to howl again.

18

As Lucas stepped through the gate, a huge gray-brown dog began to snarl, hurling itself to the end of its chain until the collar almost seemed to choke it. "Hi, baby," the cop clicked his tongue. "Good doggie," then turned to Lucas. "That's Leroy Brown," he laughed. "Come on, Leroy, roll over. Sit!"

The dog ignored the cop, slathering in rage at the stranger, like a madman in an old movie. Lucas stepped over the frozen furrows of mud until they came to the van. One headlight was gone, and the front had crumpled at one side. The windshield was a web of cracks, but still intact. "That's it," Lucas said.

"Sorry I had to drag you out here, but you got to make visual inspection before I can sign the release."

Lucas tried to open the door, but it was stuck. He peered through the window.

"No blood," the cop said. "Hey, don't worry about the kid. You could walk away from that easy. Which he did, or we would have found him. Not everybody's so lucky." He gestured at the cars around him. The Oldsmobile parked next to the van seemed to have been severed by giant wire cutters; unless the occupants were lying down, they would have been decapitated. Lucas did not look through the windows.

They passed the straining dog again, and the cop padlocked the gate behind them. The station was a giant concrete pillbox set in the middle of a block of sagging triple-deckers. They pushed open a glass door threaded with wires, and Lucas followed the cop upstairs.

"So you want the A.P.B. for running, but not the charges for unauthorized use of the vehicle. Is that right?" The cop slipped off his heavy leather jacket and searched through the papers on the desk. Lucas stood next to a chair stacked with books. On the green plastered wall below the narrow slit of window, someone had scotch-taped a hand-lettered sign: FORT APACHE.

"Yeah, I don't want him in a Secure Facility. He's not a hard kid."

"Not yet." The cop bent to his typewriter and began pecking rapidly with two fingers. "But we'll have to book him on driving without a license."

"That isn't a felony, is it?"

"No. Neither is car theft in this state, believe it or not. Which may account for the fact that this is the car theft capital of the United States. Hell, they probably wouldn't put him in a D center for that either." He typed without looking up at Lucas. "They're so full they got 'em sleeping on army cots in the halls. Can I ask you a personal question?" He squinted down at the form.

"Sure," Lucas said.

"How long you been a social worker?"

"Just under a year. Is it that obvious?"

The cop laughed. "Yeah, it is. Don't get me wrong, some of those kids are good kids basically. But you're not

115

gonna get anywhere being easy on them. You really not doing them any favor in the long run." He paused. "See, it's like there something missing up here." He tapped his forehead. "Not smarts. Some of them got a lot of smarts. My sister-in-law had a foster kid for a while. One of those longhair priests talked her into it. That kid had a lot going for him, believe me. Bright — he could get an A every time he felt like studying. Good-looking kid, too, a great talker. He could have sold you the Mystic River Bridge. Eileen really loved that kid, I mean it was 'my son' this and 'my son' that, and they got a lawyer to adopt him.

"And then, bingo. The kid disappears. He turns up in L.A. about two months later, and he don't want to have nothin' to do with Eileen and Jack no more. Broke her heart.

"Sure, I was burned up at the time, but you can't really blame the kid. He just didn't have it. He couldn't get close to you. It's like, if you didn't get it from your mother or somebody when you were little, you never do. There's always going to be something missing. You can get attached to them, but they can't get attached to you. By the time they get to be ten or twelve, it's too late. They just have to make it alone. You want kids, go get married and have your own kids."

Lucas said nothing.

"He'll be okay. You check the arcades, the fast-food joints, bus station?" the cop asked.

"Yeah," Lucas said. "I've been looking for two days."

"Then don't sweat it. He'll turn up. It's cold. He'll be back."

"You'll call me if you find him?" Lucas asked. "You won't put him in the lockup?"

"Hell, no," the cop laughed. "I'm not gonna keep fairy-bait like that around here. No, he'll be all yours. But I think you'll find him a lot faster than we do."

"Good luck," Lucas said.

"Same to you."

Lucas walked slowly down the stairs and pushed open the heavy door. In the cold air, Leroy Brown's barking echoed off the concrete walls.

The sector car from Station 3 pulled out of the parking lot beside Arthur Treacher's Fish and Chips and down the dark street that served as a shortcut to Blue Hill Ave.

The headlights caught the red retinas of animal eyes.

"Jasus, what is it?" the driver shouted.

The animal froze for an instant in the lights, then bounded off wildly.

The driver's partner was out on the passenger side and pulled his service revolver out of the stiff leather holster. It came out with a jerk. But the heavy flashlight was still on the front seat.

"Can you see him?"

"Yeah, it's him all right. Turn on the spotter!"

"I got him! I got him!"

The man put his hands together on the butt of the .38 and fired once. It recoiled up.

The sector car stood in the middle of the street, both doors open, the bright interior lights flooding onto the pavement. The radio crackled on unheard.

"That's no wolf, you eejit!" The older man laughed. "It's an Alsatian! German shepherd, you call them," he corrected himself. "You bloody fool Ginny." He laughed and thumped his partner across the shoulders.

"How the hell am I supposed to know? You think we got wolves in East Boston?"

"We haven't got wolves in Kerry neither, not the four-legged kind anyway, but I do know a dog when I see one," the man laughed.

"He looked white in the lights."

"Well of course. Don't you know all cats are gray at night? Come on now, you take the hind legs." The older man grabbed the dog's front paws.

"No way. There's shit all over here," the younger man complained.

"Poor old sod." The older man dragged the dog over to the sidewalk, and heaved the hindquarters onto the curbstone.

"There won't be a live dog out here in a few nights at this rate," the man from Kerry said as he slid his stomach behind the wheel.

"Look, I made a *mistake*," his partner grumbled.

"Probably the best thing ever happened to this neighborhood. Dogs could do with a bit of thinning out if you ask me. Like rabbits they are."

The driver released the brake, and the sector car rolled away. When the noise and lights were gone, the wolf stepped softly from behind the row of empty trash cans, and approached the dead dog. Its scent was warm and full of life. Carefully, the wolf licked up a spatter of warm blood from the curbstone and circled the kill, testing the air. Then he crouched and laid open the belly, skinned the slippery membranes off the intestines, and ate.

When the wolf was satisfied, he lapped at the water in the gutter and gathered himself to move on, looking for a lay-up.

As he reached the avenue, the sky had grayed behind the rows of low apartment buildings. The traffic was now at its lowest ebb. An ambulance passed, the siren tempting him to wail, but he was still unsure of his territory and afraid. Around the storm drains, threads of ice slivered the water, and the concrete was rough and cold under his foot pads.

The wolf raised his head and tested the smells. Among the city scents came the acrid whiff of raccoon and the doggy wet smell of fox. The wolf pricked up his ears and turned toward the wild animal smells. Just at the edge of his vision against the gray sky stood a ragged line of bare trees. He stood and looked at them for a long time before he crossed the street.

19 🔥🔥🔥

The cellar under Channing Unitarian-Universalist Church where Tony slept had been a coop run by John Talltowers, the handyman, until a month before Tony came. The huge gray space was still filled with cots where cops and private security guards and night shift workers from the Edison plant had slept fitfully and coughed and snored, wakened at intervals by alarm clocks to phone in the call box and the pay phone at the all-night drugstore across the street.

But in the first hours of a cold Sunday morning, some kids had set fire to the dumpster behind the church, and the smoke had sent the men staggering dazed into the empty parking lot. Across the street, a news photographer on night duty buying No-Doz heard the commotion, ran out with his Nikon and caught the image of the leather-jacketed cops, the cots, the police radio, and the handyman John Talltowers, for the Monday front page of the *Herald-American*. So the coop was busted.

Now John Talltowers (when the free shelters were full) had only drunks and deinstitutionalized crazies over night — and an occasional kid.

Tony almost liked John Talltowers, even though he was a loony. On nights when nobody else was in the cellar, his presence, dozing in a rump-sprung armchair by the huge octopus-armed furnace, was comforting. The old man's hair was white and shoulder-length, his strong face framed in a huge Santa Claus beard. If Tony had believed in God, he would have imagined a clean, sane John Talltowers who loved and protected him. But Tony was not a believer.

Even at three or four in the morning, John Talltowers was usually awake, smoking and reading paperbacks with the covers ripped off, the transistor on the floor tuned to the all-news station.

The voice from the radio woke Tony slowly. For a moment, he could not place it. Then he remembered.

"We have about fifty volunteers at the moment," the voice said. "Can I give you that number again over the air?"

"Sure, go ahead," the announcer spoke.

Lucas read the phone number twice. "Somebody from Friends of the Wolf will take your information and coordinate it with other sightings."

"Now suppose a volunteer does want to donate some time to your organization," the announcer said. "What would that entail? Are your volunteers armed?"

"Certainly not," Lucas spoke. "We go out in teams, with a C.B., or you can just phone in, and if we get him really close we'll send in a van from the A.P.L."

"And have you had any close encounters, so to speak?" The announcer's voice sounded amused.

"Not yet, but we have some very good leads."

"Now suppose you actually capture the wolf? What happens then?" the announcer asked.

"He'll be released with his mate and pups to form a pack in the Isle Royale preserve in Michigan. We have every reason to believe they could survive there."

"I'm sorry, but that's all the time we have right now, Joseph Lucas of the Friends of the Wolf. Good luck and thank you for being your guest on All News Radio One Hundred."

"Thank you, Neil."

A woman began to sing a commercial for twenty-four-hour banking service.

Tony pulled the overcoat around his shoulders and sat up on the canvas cot. Fifty volunteers. A hotline, C.B. radios. When a kid runs away, he thought, all they do is file an A.P.B.

Feeling under the cot in the darkness, Tony's fingers touched the stiff cellophane of the last Doritos pack and opened it. He ate them slowly to make them last, pouring out the crumbs into his palm and licking them up, then licking his fingers the way Ma's cat used to lick his fingers. When he had finished, he was still hungry.

Tony lay down again with the scratchy wool of the old coat around his neck, his knees drawn up. His eyes were used to the darkness. Through the grate in the belly of the enormous furnace, the gas pilot shone softly blue.

Wind blew under the door, ruffling the newspaper clippings about UFOs that Talltowers had taped to the cinderblock walls. The old man started, opening his eyes. "Going somewhere?" He glared at Tony.

"No. Too cold out there," Tony whispered from habit.

Talltowers listened to the static and mutter of the transistor radio. "Murder and rape, that's all they have on there," he shook his head. "And they don't tell the half of it. Now wolves. Beware of false prophets. For they come dressed as lambs, but inside they are ravening wolves."

"I know that guy, Lucas," Tony said. "He was a housefather in the group home."

Talltowers shook his head. "Social worker," he spat out the word. "Did he give you pills? Did you take them?"

"I took pills in the other place, before I went there," Tony said.

"Never take the pills, son," Talltowers advised. "Hold them under your tongue and expectorate them in the crapper. Ravening wolves," he murmured.

"I never flush 'em," Tony shook his head. "You can trade 'em on the street."

"They give you vitamins?" Talltowers sat upright, fixing him with his Almighty God stare.

"Yeah. Vitamins can't hurt you."

"That's what *you* thought," Talltowers snorted. "They knew you might not take the others, thinking they were poison. They realized you possessed some native intelligence, young man. Then you fell right into their trap and took the *real* thing! The pills that destroy the will, the will to freedom. Never take *anything!* Do you hear me? Never! Wolves come to prey upon the wolves," he muttered. "Wolves and jackals will prey upon us in our desolation. There will be not one stone left atop another, so great will be the desolation. Because you would not listen. The Abomination and the Desolation." Talltower's voice dropped to a whisper, then the lips moved silently.

Tony laid his head back on the rolled-up shirt. At Ma's house he would have cried if he had felt so terrible, but now the tears never came. Maybe, he thought, something inside him had dried up. Maybe it was the pills. Perhaps they dried up your feelings the way nose drops dried up your nose. Until hunger or cold or loneliness didn't matter anymore. He settled down to wait for dawn.

The wolf stepped carefully over the shards of broken glass out the open door of the car, where he had slept among the ashes of the charred back seat. He shook himself thoroughly, shaking the gray powder dust away. From the wooded hilltop, he looked down over the land. To the south lay more woods and an open space of empty meadow, the dead grass cropped short around small artificial hills — each with a tiny round hole in the top surmounted by a metal stick. There the fox and rabbit scent was strong.

Just below the hilltop stretched an area that held more man smell. Inside an iron fence, broken in several places, ran a long concrete walk. At the end of the walk, white columns of stone towered as high as the oldest elms. At dusk, the wolf had seen men wrapping a chain around the iron gate between the columns and fastening a padlock between the links. But the men and animals who frequented the place at night were not inconvenienced by those men's ritual.

The woods were a fifty-year-old stand of oak and elm. Leather leaves lay on the ground in clumps among the trash, spiked with dead mullein and the knobby stems of ragweed bushes bent double. Where the trees were sparse on the hill's sloping edge, bare fuzzy stalks of black-eyed Susan poked dead cones through the tangles of dried briars. The plantain leaves stood frozen stiff and green, as if the first frost had touched them only yesterday, and not five months ago.

There was still no snow.

The wolf preferred to hunt at night, but he was hungry now. Just below the hill, a fence surrounded a construction site, where work had stopped at the first frost. On either side of the huge hole, brown mounds of boulders and earth towered over the low trailers. In the cold wind, dust ghosted down the slopes. Between the two tallest mounds, a board sign announced: THE ANIMALS ARE COMING BACK TO FRANKLIN PARK.

Wind from the north carried the cow-manure smell of the hoofed stock penned on the hill across the park: wild sheep, zebras, antelopes, white-tailed deer. And on top of each chain-link fence the barbed wire angled downwards. The building gates that led to the heated shelters were open only in the day, when men were everywhere.

Above the wolf, crows called to each other, as if urging him along. The wind shifted, and brought to him the sharper fowl smell and the hoarse whistles, hoots and screeches of exotic birds. The wolf trotted down, with the crows following, flapping from one tree to another.

The old stucco Bird House was closed for the winter, but, across the stone terrace, the hardier birds wintered out in a great iron-ribbed cage covered with mesh. In the sunlight the birds crowded around aluminum pans full of raw fruits and seeds, scattering food carelessly in the dirt. Just outside the mesh, house sparrows scuffled desperately for the scraps that the captive birds' feet shoved through the wire.

The wolf flattened himself in the shade of a pine and waited. Outside the cage, a male peacock with clipped flight feathers strutted in the sun, his head bobbing like a chicken, dragging his tailfeathers through the dust. Two brown peahens lay comfortably where the sun had warmed the dirt. The peacock's size and gait brought to the wolf the image of the white farm turkeys, and he shivered with pleasure. The wolf knew how to take this prey.

Nearing the females, the peacock turned in a sliding motion and began his display, opening the tailfeathers like a fan. In the sunlight, he was instantly transfigured, the light glancing off the quivering iridescence of blue and green. The peacock held his feathers erect, the down behind his fan puffed up, and scratched backwards in the dirt.

The wolf's hindquarters quivered. As the peacock turned to face the hens, the wolf was on him. The blue neck snapped back soundlessly. Staring, the peahens stood up, too dulled by captivity to run away. Only the crows overhead burst into alarm calls.

The wolf gripped his prey tightly around the abdomen and skirted the frozen pond, dragging tailfeathers through the leaves. Panting, the wolf set down his kill near the door. But from behind, a thin raccoon, the fur missing around its muzzle and bare red skin showing along its shoulder blades, darted at him, scratching at his kill. The wolf whirled and bared his teeth, snapping at the raccoon's exposed flank. The wolf tasted blood and suddenly caught the rank smell of sickness. He drew back, afraid. The wolf shook himself, trying to rid himself of the odor.

Crows dropped down one by one around the kill. Irritated, the wolf snapped at one, but it stayed well out of reach, cocking its head from side to side. Only when the smell of the diseased coon dissipated did the wolf begin to eat.

20

The house rules said lights out at ten o'clock. When Lucas was on duty, they were. By the time he had taken a long shower (if there was still hot water in the tank and shampoo left in the bottle), scoured out the tub and picked the wet towels off the floor and cleaned the acne medications off the counter, the house would be relatively quiet. On a good night, when there were no major fights, it was a peaceful time. Lucas would make coffee, and settle in the parlor armchair with the cat, reading until he dozed.

When ten-thirty passed, and Lucas still had not walked into the TV room and shouted, "Time, gentlemen, time," the kids downstairs began to wonder. Kendo, always in training, had gone to bed at nine.

"Don't tell him, man. You stupid or somethin'?" Jerry said.

"Maybe he's sick," Sean said, and pointed upstairs.

"Shut up, man, I can't hear the TV." Kevin's arm snaked out and jabbed his brother's ribs.

Sean's leg kicked back automatically, but Kevin ducked him. Sean threw the chair aside and stalked out like an angry cat, slamming the door back against the wall.

"Don't tell him, man." Jerry did not take his eyes from the TV set. On the bright screen a red Chevy hurtled from a road and flew briefly over a riverbank.

Sean climbed the long staircase in the half-darkness, listening to the elm creak against the house in the night wind.

Lucas stood in the hall next to the telephone, his back against the wall and his eyes shut.

"Hey, you okay, Mister Lucas?" Sean asked him.

"Oh sure," Lucas said.

"You sick or something?"

Lucas picked up the battered Yellow Pages from the hall stand and hurled it at the opposite wall.

"Hey man what I *do?*" Sean asked.

"Nothing! You didn't do *anything!*" Lucas breathed. "That was a good sighting. Two nights in a row, *right* where he ought to be, and I can't *go*. I'm on duty tonight and Jay has the flu."

"Can't you get somebody else?" Sean asked.

"That was my last volunteer number. No answer. It's Saturday night." Lucas slid down with his back against the wall until he sat on the floor. "It was a big deal a couple of months ago. Now it isn't news anymore, so the hell with it. Anyway, what the hell are we doing looking for an *animal*, when we can't find Tony? He's a human being, for Chrissake!"

In the quiet, wind rattled the old wooden windowframes. At the end of the hallway, the radiator clanked.

"Doesn't that ever bother you?" he asked Sean. "You ever wonder why people care more about animals than you kids?"

"Don't bother me none," Sean shrugged. "They don't want to mess with us cause they scared of us. Nobody ever got mugged by no dog, know what I mean? It's bogus, all right, but what you gonna do about it, huh? Nothin'."

"Yeah, nothing," Lucas said. "Well, it bothers me. It bothers the hell out of me."

"Yeah, you sweat stuff too much, know what I mean?" Sean observed. "I don' know why you feel bad about stuff that ain't your fault. It's really weird, man." Sean eased himself cross-legged onto the floor where the wall-to-wall fireproof carpeting the state regs required had frayed and loosened at the edges like an old sweater. Sean picked idly at the loops.

"Where do you think Tony is?" Lucas asked.

"He's okay. Probably with friends. Cigarette?" Sean asked.

"I quit. But sometimes there are exceptions." Lucas fingered the cigarette.

"It's just tobacco, man," Sean smiled.

"No shit? I thought it was pure heroin." Lucas drew the smoke deep into his chest.

"I can get you that too but it'll cost you." Sean shrugged.

"You know, I used to wonder why so many people did drugs around here," Lucas said. "Now I wonder why more people don't."

"That's the way it is," Sean said. "You can't change nothin'."

"I disagree. I think you can." Lucas searched the hall briefly for an ashtray, then used the cellophane wrapper from the pack.

"If you wanna look for the wolf, you go." Sean tapped his ash off. Lucas noticed the homemade tattoo was fading on the boy's hand. Lucas could still read the blue lettering, BORN TO DIE, but the red dice were now pale pink blobs under the scar tissue.

"If anything happens when this place isn't covered, I'll get canned. You know that," Lucas said.

"So? Nothing happens, that's all. Anybody calls for you, you're asleep."

Lucas shook his head. "I can't. It's the kind of street where you have to watch your back, keep your guard up. Over below Forest Hills station."

"I'll go with yous. We used to live over there. They ain't so bad like they think. Dipsticks," he said softly.

Lucas stared at Sean.

"We wanna help, man, but you never ask us. You think we all babies or somethin'. We know the streets better than them volunteers," Sean snorted. "But you never ask us."

"I can't ask you," Lucas answered. "If you got hurt, I'd be responsible. It's my job to take care of you."

"So who's to know we were looking for a wolf, huh?" Sean asked. "Who's to know we ain't just messin' around? Kids onna street all the time and nobody say nothin' about it."

Lucas stared again at the skinny face framed in long dirty hair.

"Why do you want to help?" Lucas asked.

"Man, you always gotta have a *reason*," Sean laughed. "Why not? I mean, you don' have no reason neither? Do you? He ain't even your wolf."

"Yeah, I guess that's true," Lucas said.

"Okay, let's *go* man," Sean said.

They faced each other, eyes level. "Okay," Lucas said softly. "Get your coat."

"You give it back for now, okay?" Sean flipped his fingers, imitating a switchblade opening.

"I don't have it, Sean. I turned it in."

"You carryin'?" Sean asked.

"No, I don't own a gun."

Sean sighed. "Next time we take Kendo too, okay?" He rose and disappeared into his room.

Lucas turned off the hall light and glanced out the window. Above the chimney on the house across the street, the thin backward *C* of a new moon hung against a blue-black sky. "Going down to zero tonight," Lucas said aloud. "Wonder when it will snow."

A fire engine sounded thinly in the distance. Downhill a dog howled, the sound blanketing the street noises. For a moment, Lucas listened, then shrugged. It was only a dog.

The moon had not risen far when Sean and Lucas walked down the empty street in Forest Hills, back to where Lucas had parked the van. But it was no longer there.

Lucas stood looking at the empty space between the Plymouth Volare with a trash bag taped across the missing side window, and the brown Chevy pickup.

"Somebody ripped it off," Sean said.

"Brilliant deduction, Watson," Lucas said bitterly.

Lucas looked around. The same triple-deckers, the same boarded up Seven-Eleven on the corner. A cat darted warily across the street and slid under the broken lattice of a front porch. Sean hunched over, digging his hands deeper into his jacket pockets.

"You should have worn your other coat," Lucas said.

In the windows on the street, blue television lights flickered like dying fires. But the street was empty. There was no sign of the wolf.

"Christ, we couldn't have been gone more than fifteen minutes." Lucas kicked at an empty beer can. It rolled crazily down the asphalt in the cold, still air.

"It don't take long if you know your business." Sean spat onto the sidewalk.

"Who the hell would be out stealing cars on a night like this?" Lucas asked.

"Stealing vans," Sean corrected him. "Most kids, they just steal the one thing. You get real good at the one thing. Vans are very good now. You can paint stuff onna side. I saw one downtown with a naked lady holding a spear and a lion with them big fangs, and a flying dragon on the other side. Very slick," he added.

Lucas stared at the empty space, as if the van might magically reappear. "Who's going to paint naked ladies on that piece of junk?" he asked.

"Who knows, man? You couldn't hardly tell it was that beat up in the dark. You couldn't see the side where Tony did a number on it."

In the light of the red globe on the corner, Lucas checked his watch. Cold gnawed at the bare flesh between the cuffs of his coat and his woolen gloves.

Lucas fished his wallet from his pants pocket and opened it. One dollar. And some change in the other pocket. "You got any money?" he asked.

"Nothin', man. I left my wallet up to the house."

"We don't have enough for a cab. Even if we could *get* a cab." Lucas kicked at a beer can, sending it skittering over the frozen trash that had lodged in a storm drain.

There was a stillness in the cold street that frightened Lucas more than anything he had encountered in the wilderness.

"If you call the cops, they give you a ride." Sean

nodded his head toward the space where the van had been. "You gotta report it anyway or you can't get no insurance money."

"That could take hours. We gotta get back to cover the house if somebody calls."

"Take the MBTA," Sean suggested. "It ain't midnight yet."

"Yeah," Lucas nodded. "Good thinking. You know which way to go?"

"Sure man, I grew up here. We used to live about three streets over." Sean straightened out of his slouch. "The car yard's over there. We used to go in the buses and party and cut up the seats. Kid stuff."

"Yeah, kid stuff," Lucas said.

Side by side, they started down the dark street.

In the darkness, Sean and Lucas picked their way up the long stairway to the elevated platform.

At the end of the platform farthest from the change booth stood a knot of kids in Barracuta jackets. Disco music pounded faintly from a suitcase-sized boom box the biggest kid held in front of him.

The wind swirled the trash between the tracks into dust devils. DANGER THIRD RAIL ALIVE! A pigeon had roosted on the sign, its head tucked under one wing.

Above Lucas's head, the white concrete overhang was lettered with the smoke of cigarette lighters: *M.J., DISCO SUX! C.R. EATS IT, '81 BEST*, a schematic drawing of a female with gigantic breasts, her pubis covered with penciled hairs. Higher up, the black marks blurred into illegible scrawls, like smoke streaks from grease lamps in an ancient cave.

"Hey, Shuaawn," a voice half-sang, half-whispered. "Hey, who's your new friend, huh? Where's your baby brother?"

Sean froze into position slouched against the wall. He said nothing.

"You know these clowns?" Lucas asked. He drew himself up, a head taller than the biggest kid.

"Yeah, I know them," Sean whispered. It was the first time Lucas had seen him unable to conceal fear.

There was still no train. Lucas glanced around, but the starter was not on the platform.

"How come you don't introduce us?" A kid with a navy watch cap pulled over his long red hair walked toward them, a little ahead of the others. They walked closely, shoulders almost touching, the way Lucas had seen the kids in his house close ranks against outsiders. The disco music surrounded them, establishing an invisible fence.

"I'm Joe Lucas," Lucas pitched his voice just over the sound. "I'm his friend."

"Hey, man, I didn't know you had no friends." The redhead stared up at Lucas, then spat on the platform. "You ain't got friends around here, Sean. You remember *why*, Sean?"

"Leave me alone," Sean whispered.

Lucas looked down at their soft faces. Only one had the fuzz of a new mustache along his upper lip. They were just children. Young enough to be his own sons. "Why don't you knock off this TV-cop-show bravado and go home?" he wanted to say. But they would not have understood. The TV and a half-mile of old streets were their entire universe.

Behind the redhead, the boy with the fuzz of mustache began to flick a cigarette lighter on and off. There was still no train.

"Leave me alone," Sean said again like an incantation.

"Want a light?" The kid with the mustache flicked the lighter on and off near the sleeve of Sean's coat.

"Hey, watch out!" The redhead pointed at the tracks. As Lucas turned to look, the mustached kid grabbed Sean's arm and shoved the fire at his face.

"Eat it," the mustached kid yelled at Sean.

"Cut that out, you little punk!" Lucas knocked the lighter from his hand, grabbed his coat front, and shook the mustached kid.

Sean began to run. He stumbled and plunged toward the stairs. For a moment, the kids surrounded Lucas without touching him. Then the redhead turned, and struck him in the ribs. The blow felt as light as a child playfighting.

From the edge of the platform came the metal scream of an incoming train rounding a curve. Doors slid open.

Then the kids were gone, the sound of the box fading like a siren in the night.

As Lucas turned to look for Sean, weight suddenly crushed against his chest. His breath would not come. "Help me," he mouthed. "I'm having a heart attack. Help me."

Light poured onto the platform, and Lucas saw that the car was full of people.

"Oh God, I'm only thirty-five," Lucas mouthed. Pain seared through his shoulder and down his arm.

As he went to his knees, one foot felt warm and wet. Lucas stared at it as if it belonged to someone else. As the ankle turned, the shoe tilted and spilled the pavement catsup red with bright arterial blood.

21

The night wind brought the wolf the smell of man and death at the same time, just as he rounded the knoll above the golf course. He froze. The only sounds were the white-footed mice scuttling through their tunnels under the dead leaves, and the constant whine of cars on Blue Hill Avenue. Slowly, he tested the air, then trotted downhill, pausing to scratch at his muzzle with one forepaw.

The itch was like the feel of his winter coat under the guard hairs on the first warm days of spring, but no amount of rubbing relieved it. The wolf sat on his hip and scratched at the spot with the long toenails on one hind paw until blood came, but the itching was still there. He stood up and shook himself as if he were wet, then went on.

The man hung suspended from a swamp oak branch in

the thickest stand of forest, the same place where the wolf had often found dead dogs and cats, and once a dead horse being dragged from a pickup truck. On the ground beneath the man, an envelope carefully weighed down with a rock fluttered in the night air.

The wolf crouched, still uncertain, in a stand of bare sumac bush. He had never seen a man in a tree before. The unknown was always suspect. Yet the smell of meat was plain, and he was hungry.

For the first time, his mind connected the smell of man with prey. It was a new and compelling thought, for his range was full of man, and he was always hungry.

Stalking downwind, the wolf worked in closer to the tree. In the half-light of the crescent moon, he studied the figure carefully. The ankles above the shoe tops were swollen. Otherwise, the body seemed whole, untainted, and harmless. On his belly, the wolf crawled to within a few feet of the hanging shape.

He paused, then launched himself into the air, snapping at one leg. His teeth closed on the pleat of one pant leg, and he dropped to the ground. Above him, the push that the wolf gave the body started the figure swaying in the moonlight as if it had come to life.

Terrified, the wolf bolted up the hillside and into an evergreen thicket. He shivered and crouched deep among the branches.

Far below, the hanged man swayed slowly, turning in half-circles as the momentum of the push died away. None of the animals who scavenged there dared touch it.

When Tony came out of the cold and stepped on the mat, the doors to the Emergency Room opened the way a supermarket door opens, but they slid into the walls instead of swinging out. The outer room was filled with wooden benches like pews in a church, and on the benches people waited and smoked, or sat with head in hands. A few slept, heads lolling back. In the farthest corner, a bald woman crocheted the edges of an old army blanket with bright purple variegated yarn while she talked aloud to no one.

"Oh Jesus, oh my sweet Jesus," someone moaned. "Oh my sweet Jesus, I done wrong."

Tony stood near the doors for a moment, letting the warmth spread to his fingers and toes, and watched what the others did. First, he noticed they spoke to a black man behind the desk and then received a slip of paper. Later, a white woman in a lab coat and stethoscope called out names. When the rear door opened, Tony caught a glimpse of a long hallway partitioned into cubicles with green plastic shower curtains. A folded wheelchair stood against the doorframe.

Behind him, the doors snapped back, and Tony jumped to the side. Four black men in dungarees carried a stretcher with an I.V. bottle dangling from a pole. "Come on, baby, move it," one of them shouted.

Tony closed his eyes. If he had been driven to one of the hospital doors, he might have thought that he could find Lucas by chance. But Tony had walked all the way. For five or six blocks, he had been able to size up the enormous old brick and new concrete and steel complex, a miniature city extending over a street and linked with plastic-walled pathways.

There was no hope of sneaking in and finding Lucas. So Tony had thought up a story. But even in his mind, he could not say it.

At the desk, a young black woman in a bright orange sweater and cornrowed hair looked down at him.

"Could I have Joseph Lucas's room number please?" Tony asked casually.

"Oh sweet Jesus, I done wrong," a voice moaned behind him.

"I'll call Admissions," the woman spoke in a clipped West Indian accent. "Did you know that visiting hours end at eight?"

Tony nodded. Visiting hours. He hadn't thought of that.

The woman pushed buttons swiftly on a small white console.

"Room two-ten. B wing. Young man, visiting hours are over. You can't see him now. Is an adult with you?"

From nowhere, a security guard appeared, approaching Tony.

"Please, lady," Tony's words came out thick and awkward. "Please, I just want to see him."

"Visiting hours are from ten to twelve and six to eight," she said.

"I have to see him because he's . . ." Tony stopped, trying to say the word aloud. He had said it easily when he was little, at every placement. It came hard now.

"Are you all right?" the woman asked.

"Please let me see him," Tony said. "Please. He's my father."

Pain woke Lucas in slow stages. He stirred under the coarse sheet, feeling his body grow aware. At first, the pain seemed only an irritation that would pass and let him sleep again, but, as consciousness returned, it strengthened. Lucas put a hand experimentally to his side and touched the stiff bandage. Memory came back slowly: hot lights, noise, a hand in a latex glove stabbing into his side.

Lucas held his breath and began to count. Panting, he shifted position from right to left, side to side, yet the pain held in all positions.

Lucas reached for his glasses on the bedside tray-table. He let the arm fall, exhausted by the effort. Hot tears forced themselves under his eyelids.

"Your son is here to see you," a woman's voice said.

Lucas opened his mouth to say that he had no son, when he recognized the slouching, skinny body and the black mass of hair. The face was blurred, but he knew it. "Okay," Lucas whispered.

Tony hung back in the doorway and stared at the long body moving awkwardly under the sheet.

"Take it easy, I've got your medication right here." The nurse set the small tray down, raised the hypo to the light, and delicately flicked the point with one finger. "Take it easy," she said. "Try to hold still."

"I can't," Lucas whispered. "I can't."

Tony looked at the white curve of the man's buttocks

as she pushed aside the hospital johnny. He winced as the needle sank in. She rubbed the spot briefly with the heel of her hand, and tucked the sheet back in.

Tony saw that Lucas's body was trembling.

"Are you okay?" Tony whispered.

"Yeah," Lucas mouthed. His eyes were shut now. All the color had gone from his face, and the stubble of beard showed black around his chin and down his neck. Only the thick curly hair seemed the same, Tony thought.

Lucas lay still now under the sheet, one arm flung to the side. Tony touched the hand to tuck it inside; the fingers felt cold. Carefully, he unfolded the thermal blanket at the foot of the bed and pulled it over Lucas, tucking the edges in the way Ma had taught him to make his bed.

"Please don't die," Tony said.

Lucas opened his eyes. "I'm not planning on it," he murmured, slurring the words as if he were drunk. He licked his lips, and Tony could see the skin had cracked into red sores.

Tony looked away. "You need anything?"

Lucas shook his head. "Could you stay a minute?" he asked slowly.

"Sure. I can stay. I got plenty of time."

Tony pulled the only chair in the room up beside the high bed and sat down. Next to the bed was a tray-table on wheels and a small dresser. Under the small window stood a radiator with peeling silver paint.

"Could you turn off the light? It hurts my eyes." Lucas licked his lips again.

Tony reached up and snapped the switch. Even without

the light, the room had enough illumination from the nurses' station across the corridor for Tony to see. Tony unscrewed the top to the water bottle, wet a piece of Kleenex, and dabbed it gently on Lucas's mouth over the raw skin.

"Is that better?" Tony asked. "You want me to get you something to drink?"

Lucas turned his face away, and Tony saw it had screwed up as though he were crying.

"What's the matter? Did I hurt you?" Tony asked.

Lucas shook his head. Gradually, his breathing evened out again. For a while, they listened to the people go by, the click of a telephone dialing, and the sirens. There was a short burst of laughter from the nurses' station, then quiet again.

"How did you know I was here, Tony?" Lucas said more clearly.

"I heard it over the radio. I figured you could use some help."

"You were right," Lucas said. "Thanks."

"Hey don' worry about it," Tony shrugged.

Lucas face turned back toward him, eyes closed again. Under the blanket, his chest rose and fell like a machine. When Tony was sure he was asleep, he stood up. But Lucas was still awake.

"Tony, would you think about coming back?" Lucas said slowly, but the words were clear.

Tony stood still, not answering.

He stared down at the lump where Lucas's feet stuck up. "Would I have to go to school?"

"Yeah, and the therapy group. The whole shooting match. You don't have to tell me now. Just think about it. Okay?"

"I was thinking about it anyway," Tony said. "You get cold bumming around this time of year."

"Yeah, I can see that," Lucas said.

Tony pushed the chair closer to the head of the bed and sat down. "You find the wolf yet?" he asked.

"No, but we'll keep trying," Lucas murmured, his voice fading out again. His eyelids fluttered, and then closed.

Tony drew the white blanket farther up over Lucas's shoulders, but this time he did not stir. Tony watched him. Under the hair that had fallen over his forehead, Lucas's eyelids twitched in the first dreaming stage of sleep.

Tony smoothed Lucas's hair back, and sat down again to wait.

22

"Vinnie Boudreau?" A young man in a down parka over coveralls walked up to Vinnie's camper as they struggled to get the last deer down the wooden ramp.

"Yeah, that's me." Vinnie ducked to avoid a kick in the side and shoved the animal in the chest. It twisted and snorted in the cold air, and finally plunged down the slope, head down, into the waiting transport cage.

"Can I talk to you a minute when you're done?"

"Sure. This here's the last one." Vinnie wiped his hands on his pants, and bent to help the two men and a girl remove the ramp.

"I thought you told me that deer was always so quiet?" the girl said.

"She is," Vinnie answered. "It's the weather. They can smell a storm coming, and it spooks them."

"You really believe that?" the girl asked.

"They may be sensitive to the pressure changes." The man in the down parka stared up at the low gray clouds. "It's been a funny winter with no snow."

"Open fields in winter, full burying ground in spring, they used to say," Vinnie put in.

"Come on," the man in coveralls urged. "Let's get out of this cold."

Vinnie followed him through a huge brassbound door into the old stucco pagoda-style Bird House. The moist air inside smelled of damp earth and rotting leaves, like a greenhouse. All around him, strange whistles and hoots echoed through the walls. The carpeted corridors had been covered with newspapers, the lights dim. They passed through a glass door taped with brown paper, past a sign reading TROPICAL RAIN FOREST HABITAT and through a door marked NO ADMITTANCE.

Along three walls, the office held huge glass-fronted bookcases full of thick books. On the door a poster of "Owls of North America" had been taped. In the center of the room stood an old picnic table with benches, and, to the side, a metal office desk and filing cabinet. Vinnie glanced at the thick leather book open on the table — an engraving of a bird that looked like a giant woodcock, titled "Germain's Peacock-Pheasant."

He wondered whether or not to sit down.

"I'm Jim Stone. I run the Bird House," the man said.

"Pleased to meet you." Vinnie stood back, uncertain.

"I heard you were closing your park in Maine," Stone said.

"That's right. I had enough." Vinnie shifted from foot to foot.

"Look, I know what happened, okay? I'm not into blaming anybody. I wanted to talk to you because I thought I might have a lead on your wolf."

"Why don't you call up them Friends of the Wolf?" Vinnie said softly.

"Because I don't want a bunch of white middle-class volunteers crawling all over this park, especially at night. This park happens to be in the middle of the ghetto. We have enough trouble getting our own people in and out of here safely." Stone motioned Vinnie to the bench. "I'll get right to the point. When it isn't too cold, we usually let some of the larger birds out in winter. But this winter, in a month and a half, we lost two peacocks, three guinea fowl, and a Canada goose. My first thought was feral dogs. We got plenty of them around here. The thing that made me think of your wolf is the way he carried off his kill, instead of eating it right then and there. Dogs eat right away, or they just leave it there."

"Could be a real smart dog." Vinnie looked at the floor. "Any tracks?"

"The ground is like a rock. An elephant wouldn't leave tracks."

Vinnie did not answer immediately. When the wind gusted, the glass in the tall gilded frames rattled with the slight quiver of the old building, an animal shaking itself. Muffled whistles and wild cackling sounded for a moment, then died away.

"I think he might go to the woods, if he could find woods. I mind the first time I let him loose, he ran right off to the woods, and I thought, this is goodbye, fella! But an hour later he was back, jumping all over me." Vinnie buried his head in his hands. "I wish to God he'd a stayed gone then. That's the trouble, see? You think you can have 'em run free and have 'em love you too at the same time that they're wild, but it can't be like that. You want it that way, but it never can be."

Stone nodded. "I'll give you a call if I find anything definite, okay? You'll be the first to know."

"Okay. Thanks. I, I better be goin'," Vinnie said. "I figure this snow to be a real big one."

"Sure looks like it. Maybe we'll get you some tracks after all."

"They'd be big." Vinnie opened his hand out wide. "A wolf's tracks are as big as your hand. That's why people had the idea wolves were so big. They really aren't any bigger than a big dog, but their feet are spread out. To walk on the snow."

"Thanks. I'll keep my eye out for any tracks." Stone

closed the door behind him. Slowly, Vinnie made his way through the exhibit hallways, the strange birds gibbering around him like ghosts.

When Vinnie reached his camper, the fine snow had already begun to gather in arcs on the black pavement. White powder formed tiny dunes, then shifted, whirling close to the ground like sand. Vinnie glanced once more at the line of bare trees above him on the hill, then wrenched open the camper door against the wind.

"That ain't no twenty-five inches deep." Jerry got up and looked out the parlor window. On the large screen of the old color television set, the governor was still speaking.

"Sure is, man. Look, you can't even see the front steps across the street!" Kevin shoved his brother.

Tony joined them at the window. All he could see was whiteness, threaded with black utility wires tossing like kite strings. The house shuddered, rattling the dishes in the corner cabinet.

"At least we still got electricity," Sean said, twisting Kevin's arm.

"You picked a good time to come back, man," Jerry said to Tony. "Man, if you was onna street now, you'd be the world's first quick-frozen Ginny."

"Jesus, no school all week," Kevin said.

"All week! Hell, no school probably all month!" Jerry shouted.

"Maybe all year!" Sean added.

"Oh sure, man, we really gonna have snow in *June*." Kevin poked him.

"Who knows man?" Jerry asked. "Jesus, I never seen nothing like this."

"Looks like the set for *Ice Station Zebra*, man," Sean said.

"Ice Station Zebra Meets the Wolfman!" Jerry yelled.

"Keep it down, will you? He's asleep." Tony pointed upwards.

"Jesus, all he *does* is sleep," Jerry shrugged.

"Well, you'd sleep too if you was doped up like that!" Tony flared. "The *man* is in *pain*, stupid. He's *supposed* to *rest*."

"Hey, take it easy, man," Sean said.

They stared out at the shifting whiteness.

"You wanna try going out? See if the Handy Stop is open?" Kevin asked.

Sean began rummaging in a pile of coats in the corner. "Any of you guys got a buck?"

"You owe me from last week," Jerry said.

"Hey, Tony, get your coat!" Kevin shouted.

Tony stayed at the window. "No, you guys go. I'll cover the phone."

Kicking and scuffling, they ran out the door, letting in a burst of cold air. Then the house was quiet. There was no sound from Lucas's room upstairs. Tony stood at the window, looking out into the white, and laid his cheek against the cold glass.

23

The wolf woke when the snow stopped. Slowly, he nosed his way through the car window and floundered into the midst of a drift. In the intense cold, the snow was soft as flour. The wolf breathed in, but the snow muffled the smells. He shook himself, lapped at the snow briefly, and dug back into the car. In the recess where the back seat had been, he turned around three times and curled himself tightly, nose to tail. For the rest of the daylight hours, he slept.

When he woke again, the world had changed.

The drifts had skinned over. The wolf put one wide paw tentatively out, then another. Now the snow could bear his weight. Carefully, he stepped to the new crest of the hill, and stood testing the wind.

The city was as still now as the woods in winter. Below the wolf, over the trash and rotting leaves, spread quiet and undulating fields of blue white. Beyond the fence of naked elms, Orion the Hunter lay over the horizon, his sword belt shining with the Pleiades. Over the pink city-glow, the Great Dog glittered. Above him, a half-moon rose bone white against the sea of stars.

All around the wolf, the new snow crust sparkled hard and crystalline with ice, billions of tiny sparks fallen on the land.

The wolf threw back his head, cupped his lips over his teeth, and sang the loner's howl.

Toward the park gate, a dog wailed in answer. The wolf tested the wind and recognized a shepherd-Labrador who scavenged the alleys off the avenue. He waited. At the edge of his vision, a male Harlequin Great Dane floundered up the hill, wagging his stubby tail. Behind him, a gray sheep dog with matted fur trotted easily on the surface. The wolf waited for them to reach him.

When the pack had assembled, they greeted each other, tussling and barking, mounting each other and clasping muzzles. Their bodies felt warm against the wolf in the cold night. He rubbed shoulders with them, the pain of his hunger and the itching forgotten for a moment.

Then he led them single file downhill, strung out ten paces apart, with the Great Dane trailing behind, their moonshadows elongated blue on the snow.

The huge bird cage was empty now, the stream and pond frozen and buried deep in snow. The wolf cast about, but found only the smell of possum, stale and old. Even man-smell was dim.

Then the wind carried him the scent of the hoofed stock. The dogs bunched up and nosed around the wolf, begging. Now they were all as hungry as he. Snow had buried the trash cans and forced inside the humans who fed them. Even the cats and smaller dogs that might have become prey were shut indoors. The Great Dane whined and licked the wolf's mouth like a puppy.

The wolf turned and began to trot toward the warm smells, keeping an even pace. Behind him the dogs followed, barking and jumping with excitement.

The wolf ran lightly uphill on the crust of the snow,

along the path between the trees where broken concrete steps led to Hoofed Stock. Most of the pens, the homes of zebras and exotic deer, were empty now in the deep cold, their occupants inside the heated building in the hub of a network of chain-link fences and barbed wire.

At the third pen from the right, the wolf smelled the white-tailed deer.

The deer were sleeping the way they did in the winter yards in the forest, sheltered from the wind by evergreens: ears flat on their heads, curled nose to belly, their undercoats so thick that the snow pressed beneath them did not melt. Lulled by the cold and the hunger when men did not come to feed them, they lay silent in the winter fasting sleep. There were four does in the winter herd, three yearlings, and two bucks yarding close to the warmth of the concrete wall.

Snow had drifted against the fence until the tips of the barbed wire jutted barely two feet above the snow line.

The wolf gathered his body like a cat and easily cleared the fence. One by one, the dogs followed. The old buck who had once lived wild caught their scent first. He was slow, his teeth worn down until his cheeks had sunken in like an old man's, but he had fought before. He stood up, shook himself ready, and lowered his head. The wolf dodged aside, wary of his threatening stance. Then he circled closer to the does.

The dogs began to yelp with excitement, but the wolf was silent. The deers' sharp hooves, their only weapon, now put them at a disadvantage. They floundered in the soft snow, the broken crust tearing at their legs, while the dogs ran easily on the top, chasing them around the pen like puppies playing.

Next to the wall, the wolf cornered a panting, pregnant doe. Rearing up, she flailed at him with her hooves, but she was tiring fast. The wolf nipped her haunch, tasted blood, then darted back.

Behind her, the shepherd-Labrador fastened his teeth in her rump and jerked her backwards. The wolf laid open her abdomen, and, ripping through the uterine wall, tore out the fetus before she was dead. The pack began to feed.

At dawn, the clank of a huge machine in the distance roused the wolf. He rose heavily from the warm nest of snow where he had curled himself, and shook his coat off. Inside the pen, the deer carcasses lay scattered across the snow where they had fallen—some partially eaten, some whole but for the wounds that killed them.

The dogs sprawled meat-drunk in the snow, as if they too were dead. The wolf stared at them, but then drew back. He did not want their companionship now. Lapping bloody snow, the wolf drank until his thirst was gone, and trotted to the fence. With an effort, he cleared the barbed wire.

From the Hoofed Stock pens, the Blue Hills shone white before him in the cold pink dawn. His hunger was fully satisfied, and yet the wolf was restless. He sat and scratched at the itchy places on his skin until they oozed blood and pus. Then, without turning to look at the pack or the kill, he began to walk with a steady, loping gait toward the mountains.

The telephone half-woke Lucas from an uneasy doze. He heard running bare feet down the hall. He lay back against the musty pillow, wishing the sound would go away, but knowing that sleep would not come again. He glanced at the Percodan bottle on the dresser. But it had not been four hours.

Sun reflected off the snowbanks poured through the flimsy nylon curtains into the bedroom.

"Hey, Mister Lucas, it's for you!" Kevin sang out.

Lucas swung his legs carefully onto the floor, and eased himself up.

"You're gonna miss the bus!" he yelled back.

"Ain't no bus." Tony appeared at the door in his underwear. "Remember? No school?"

"Telephone," Kevin shouted again.

"Coming!" Lucas yelled back. He knew better than to run. Bent slightly at the waist, he shuffled down the cold corridor to the wall phone. He leaned against the wall and held the receiver against one cheek, listening.

Tony stood silently beside him.

"Is it bad news, Mr. Lucas?" he whispered.

Lucas nodded. "I'll be at the corner as soon as I get dressed," he said into the receiver. "Don't try to get up this street. It isn't plowed."

"What happened?" Tony asked. "What's the matter? Did somebody die?"

Lucas set the receiver carefully back into the cradle and covered his face with his long fingers.

"Yeah, Tony," he said. "Somebody died."

24

Captain O'Meara pulled the station wagon with the Animal Protection League logo to a stop in the middle of a plowed track, leaving the engine running. A snowmobile had passed, leaving thin tracks over the marks engraved by caterpillar tractor treads and tire chains. In the bright cold, children were climbing the snow mounds and dragging sleds with paper bags of groceries. Adults, booted and muffled like Arctic explorers, smiled and waved as they passed, as if the day were the climax of a great celebration.

Lucas came slowly down the hill with two teenaged boys while O'Meara waited. At the mound on the corner, O'Meara saw one kid reach up to help him over, but Lucas waved him away. The boys stood still, watching Lucas. Then the smaller boy continued on with him, the other walking back.

Lucas stepped awkwardly over the ridges of snow in the street and knocked his boots before getting into the car. He was breathing hard. O'Meara saw that the boy beside him was Tony.

"They didn't do your street yet?" O'Meara asked.

Lucas shook his head.

"They haven't even touched mine. I had to walk and then I got a ride in on a snowplow. They're supposed to start running the MBTA tomorrow."

"Any more news?" Lucas asked.

"They got all the dogs. Two of 'em got tags, but out of date. The wolf tracks lead up to the street and stop where it was plowed. We couldn't find any more — probably messed up by people walking.

"You feel okay?" O'Meara added.

"I'm all right. Just out of shape."

"The news people will be there before us," O'Meara warned. "I hope you got something to say to them."

The car clanked slowly along on its chains. Only one lane had been plowed, and every time another vehicle came in sight, they pulled over. At Washington Street, a snowmobile roared by them, pulling a toboggan full of shrieking children.

"I was hoping with so much other stuff going on, we might not get much coverage," Lucas said.

O'Meara shook his head. "Animal stories always get coverage. And blood gets coverage — that never ceases to amaze me. They'll send five guys to get one shot of a stiff wrapped in blankets.

"After that film hits the air, the animal lovers will go wild. They even tore the babies out of the pregnant does."

"I've heard wolves surplus-kill in the wild when the deer get snowbound and can't run away," Lucas said. "Otherwise they don't take more than they can eat."

"Maybe so," O'Meara answered. "Dogs sure don't have that control. I've seen them go through a whole flock of sheep and maybe eat one, and kill the rest. Look, I'm sorry about the wolf, but let's be realistic. Your chances of finding him and getting him alive were about nil anyway. Just thank God he didn't kill some kid."

"Wolves don't kill people," Lucas said.

"Maybe," O'Meara nodded. "Maybe not."

The station wagon waited behind a panel truck to cross Blue Hill Avenue. Lucas watched the people. A skier in a blue parka wobbled down the avenue, framed by the Big Blue. At the gates of the park, the elms were bare and snowless, but the pines and bushes bent under heavy loads.

The TV vans were already parked as close to the entrance as the plowed streets would allow.

Tony stood close to Lucas as he climbed out of the car and started up the pathway trampled in the snow. The crowd began about halfway up the slope to Hoofed Stock. Kids elbowed and pushed each other. A man laboring under a portable TV camera and a girl trailing ropes of heavy electrical wire picked their way up the slippery slope, not noticing Lucas and Tony.

Breathing hard, Lucas shoved forward, looking over the heads of the crowd.

"What are you going to say to the TV people?" Tony asked.

"Maybe you better wait here, Tony. This is going to be gross," Lucas said.

"I bet I seen worse things." Tony looked down at the trampled snow.

Lucas looked down at him for a moment. "Yeah, I guess you have," he said.

Together, they pushed past a woman carrying a baby. Lucas wedged himself next to the barbed wire that poked up through the snow. Tony peered around his shoulder, edging his body close.

A man was pulling a brown shape by the legs. The only sounds were people whispering, the *click-whirr* of the still cameras, and the crows calling overhead. At first, Tony's mind saw red paint or tile, and then realized that the snow for twenty or thirty feet around was dyed deep with blood.

Despite himself, nausea turned his stomach, and he looked away.

"Hey Mr. Lucas!" someone shouted. "Can I ask you a couple of questions?"

25

In low pockets under trees and along the sides of rocks on the Big Blue, the snow still held, soft and pitted with tiny bullet-sized holes or melted away entirely beneath a lacework of ice crust. Turtles dug out of the loosened mud with soft pops and heaved themselves up to search for mates. Under the tree roots, the tiny snakes that had slept curled around each other in tight balls began to unthread themselves and slither out over the dead leaves and skunk cabbage. Owls feasted on newborn mice. In the deer herds, it was time for the first fawns to be born and the last sick and old deer to die.

At dusk, the wolf tracked an old buck down the burnt-over section of hillside where blueberry bushes and scrub oak grew. He kept low to the ground, loping steadily until the itch became overpowering, then sat back on his haunches and dug his nails against the bare flesh around the choke collar and rubbed his muzzle back and forth on a stone until blood and tufts of fur clung to the leafless Virginia creeper vines around him.

When he returned to it, the scent trail was still good.

The buck's teeth had worn down to nubbins, and his knee joints ached with the damp that rose from the melting snow, but he trotted steadily downhill toward his nightly raid on the bales of forage stacked near the barn of the small zoo and museum at the start of the hiking trails. He could not scent the wolf downwind.

The buck paused at the edge of the highway that curved in switchbacks to the TV antennae on the mountaintop, fearful of exposing himself in the treeless space until he had tested the air. As the asphalt cooled faster than the forest floor, ground fog condensed on the black pavement, blurring vision. As the buck turned toward the woods to check once more, he caught the wolf's scent faintly, then saw the flash of white as the wolf crouched in the leafless blueberry bushes.

For an instant, they stared at each other. Then the buck plunged into the roadway with the wolf ten yards behind and closing. Sharp hooves skittered on the pavement. In the dark, the wolf gained on the old buck. Suddenly light broke over the wolf's fully dilated eyes, blinding him with whiteness. The scream of steel against steel filled the air, and then came the impact.

The phone rang four, five, six times in the dark hallway, until a hand with BORN TO DIE tattooed on it picked up the receiver. "Project Turnabout," Sean said into the receiver. "Whaddya want?"

Sean nodded sleepily, shifting from one foot to the other. He stood barefoot in jockey shorts, the tattoos on his chest like scribbles on white paper.

"Yeah, he works here. Want me to wake him up?"

"What is it?" Tony yelled from across the hall.

"It's an ob-seen caller," Jerry shouted back. "He wants to meet you at the Apollo Lounge."

"Shut up, man, this is serious. Hey, Mister Lucas!" Sean shouted down the hall. "Hey, hurry up!"

Lucas stood a moment at the phone, listening, then hung up. He held his breath, and then released it slowly. "Can you guys get breakfast and get off to school alone?"

"Sure, man." Sean grinned.

"I mean get to school. Not the arcade."

"Sure, we can take the bus."

"I gotta use the van." Lucas ran his fingers through his bushy hair. "Can I bum a cigarette?"

"What happen man?" Sean asked softly.

"They found the wolf," Lucas said tonelessly.

Sean turned his face away. "He dead. I knew it."

'Don't tell Tony, okay?" Lucas asked.

"I can handle it," Sean said.

"No arcade, okay?"

"Where was he?" Sean asked. "He make it back to Maine?"

Lucas shook his head. "The Big Blue. Remember? We went hiking there once."

Sean nodded.

"Don't tell Tony yet, okay?" Lucas asked.

26

It was still dark, but the birds had started to sing when Lucas parked the Project Turnabout van in the lot by the Trailside Museum in the Blue Hills. As he walked, he picked out their songs: *Kill 'em, cure 'em, give 'em physic*, sang the robin. *Peter, peter*, sang the cardinal. *Drink your tea-heee-heee*, sang the towhee. *Hoe it, hoe it*, sang the thrush.

As Lucas stopped to listen, he heard, for the first time in years, the chorus of the frogs, thin and delicate beyond the bare trees.

The year had come around again to spring.

Lucas stood still on the gravel driveway for a long time listening to their song.

"You Joe Lucas?" a man's voice startled him. Lucas turned to see a small man in a work shirt, dungarees, and a John Deere cap. "You like that sound too," he said softly.

"Spring peepers," Lucas answered.

The man nodded. "I never seen one close up. About this big, so they say," he measured out a fingernail. "Come on inside. It's warmer."

Lucas followed the man down the concrete steps into the basement of the Visitor Center. Inside, rows of wooden boxes, like lockers, lined the wall. Each had a glass door covered with paper. At the far end of the cellar stood a sink, hot plate, and shelves. On the drainboard a glass aquarium full of wood shavings rustled with white rats.

"I was releasing an owl when I found him." The man took off the cap, revealing a bald head. "I do the raptors. The name's Earl Johnson," he added. "Anyway, I was releasing a horned owl when I saw him. He was off the highway, but I'm pretty sure it was a road-kill. The skull was dented in — blood around the nose and mouth. Those kids drive up that road like they was bats out of hell."

"You sure it was the wolf and not a dog?" Lucas grasped at the question without hope.

"It's the wolf all right. I wouldn't feel too bad about it, though. He had the mange real bad. It's a tough way to go."

Lucas stared at the rats burrowing in the shavings, their pink feet scrabbling on the glass. All over, he told himself. All over.

"Food for these guys over here." Johnson opened one of the wooden cupboards. A small gray owl swiveled its head and stared at them with unblinking yellow eyes. "Little guy like that eats maybe five, six mice a day.

"Paper's to keep them from trying to fly through. They don't understand glass. Not too bright, owls." He tickled the owl's neck feathers with one finger. The bird chittered at him angrily, opening its beak to strike. "He's a feisty little guy, ain't you?" Johnson smiled. "You want to fight me, huh fella?

"He's too tough for me." Johnson carefully latched the cupboard door.

Lucas nodded. All over. Done.

"You want to take the body with you?" Johnson asked.

Lucas stared at him.

"I mean, I thought maybe you might want to put him in a pet cemetery. The SPCA has a real nice one. I never been there myself," he added.

Lucas remembered a pet cemetery he had seen in New York. "To My Beloved Muffin, Rest in Peace." The grass shaved close with lawnmowers like a suburban lawn.

"No, he doesn't belong in a pet cemetery. He wasn't really a pet. I'd rather bury him in the woods," Lucas said.

Johnson replaced the cap. "Suits me fine. I got a shovel in here and another one in the truck. I always carry a shovel in the truck for road-kills. See, if you leave a dead animal in the road, a fox or coon will go in after it, and you get another road-kill."

As they walked up the cellar steps, the light was stronger. The spring peepers had stopped, and now the woods were still.

Johnson handed Lucas a shovel, the tip crusted with gray clay. They walked around the otter pool, past the porcupine's enclosure, and up the trail, skirting the sloping meadow kept open for the skid trail. Sun warmed Lucas's shoulders.

Overhead, the branches were bare, but in the forest floor life was returning. The black carpet of old leaves, frozen all winter, rotted now in the warmth — pierced with shoots of skunk cabbage and bracken. The twin leaves of maple shoots sprouted thin green in tiny forests from the black ooze. Lucas turned and glimpsed a pheasant in a tangle of dead blackberry vines. The bird froze momentarily, then scuttled away.

All around him, the woods seemed frighteningly clear and perfect, the way the world had looked on the morning he had worn his first pair of glasses. Each twig stood out sharp against the background, each new bud precious and full of detail.

Johnson knelt under a low scrub oak and pulled away a branch with brown leaves still clinging to it. The wolf lay with his neck arched back and his paws extended. The black lips had pulled back, showing long white canine teeth. Clotted blood flecked the muzzle. The choke collar hung loose around the thin neck. Lucas reached out.

"Don't touch it without the gloves," Johnson warned. "People can get mange."

In gray patches the white fur had worn away. Along the flank, in one bare spot, Lucas could see the protruding arch of ribs. The pelvic bones jutted sharply at the hip, like photos of starving children. Even though he stood next to it, it seemed unreal.

Johnson shoved the spade into the softened ground. A gray squirrel scolded alarm from the tree above. Lucas picked up the other shovel, and dug it in with his foot.

The sun was warmer now, and Lucas began to sweat. Awkwardly, he undid his jacket first, then his shirt and laid them on the oak branches. Johnson glanced at the long red scar, but said nothing.

Far above them in the warm sky, a turkey vulture circled on an updraft, waiting.

"How deep do we go?" Lucas asked.

"A little more." Johnson looked over the trench. "If you just cover him up, the scavengers'll dig him up again. Might not hurt to lay on a few of them rocks too."

The men dug farther. Johnson pulled a gray rag from his pocket and mopped his face, continuing on up to the bald spot on top. Reaching into his pocket, he tossed Lucas a pair of stained gardening gloves. "Here, you take the forelegs."

Lucas lifted the wolf's front paws, surprised at the light weight. The head dangled limply down. Together, they laid it in the trench. Johnson took up his spade again, and began to throw on dirt.

The lumps of earth fell with a hollow sound on the wolf's rib cage. All the white fur was brown with dirt, and then the wolf was gone.

"There's a spigot next to the coon cage that's turned on. We can wash off there," Johnson said.

Laying the shovel aside, Johnson washed his hands in the cold water. Then Lucas stepped up to the muddy place and rinsed his hands off, throwing water on his face and neck and letting it run down his naked chest. He buttoned the shirt slowly, fingers stiff from the grip on the shovel.

All around them, the droplets on the new leaves of the blackberry vines caught the morning sun. A mockingbird flashed past, white at the tail.

Crunching the dead leaves, Johnson walked down the path. Lucas followed slowly, then stopped. From below came the voices of his kids. For a moment, Lucas was confused, doubting his hearing. Then anger welled up in him.

Leaning on the fence around the otter pool, Kevin and Sean in their *Leprechaun Tap* jackets watched the otters. Tony was laughing at Jerry leaning out over the railing. Kendo, tall and straight in his martial arts jacket, watched with his arms folded, his shaven head gleaming black as polished wood in the sun.

"Hey, look at that sucker dive! Man, he's like a fuckin' submarine." Jerry pointed at the animals rolling in the water.

"Man they look like giant rats!" Kevin leaned over the railing.

"Ah-ooo-gah! Ah-ooo-gah! Dive, Dive! We're under attack!"

"You push me and you dead, man!" Sean ducked back.

Lucas stared past them to the parking lot. Beside the van sat a gray Oldsmobile Cutlass Supreme with wire wheels.

"If they hot-wired that car, I'm gonna kick ass from here to Dorchester," Lucas breathed.

Jerry waved as he approached, and smiled engagingly. "Hey, Mistah Lucas, we didn't steal this car. We borrowed it from my brother."

"Hey come on, man, he didn't *say* you stole it." Brian nudged him.

"I could feel the *paranoia*," Jerry drew out the long word.

"Does your brother know you borrowed it?" Lucas said evenly.

"Sure man, I told him it was for a funeral. You know all us Italo-Americans are queer for funerals."

Kevin began to whistle the theme song from *The Godfather*.

"Don't shit him, man, we know all you Greaseballs do is tie a couple of cinder blocks to the stiff and dump him offa Revere Beach Parkway at high tide." Sean grabbed his brother's arm.

"All right already," Lucas said. "So which of you clowns has a valid driver's license?"

Jerry dug into his jeans pocket and presented a worn scrap of paper. "It's a learner's permit," he said. "My brother's teaching me."

Lucas studied it. "This expired eight months ago. Look, see those numbers where it says EXPIRES?"

Jerry nodded.

"No, look at it. How are you going to learn to read looking at *me*, huh? See, the first number stands for the month. January is one, February is two, got that?"

Jerry fidgeted. "Sure, man."

"Okay, so what month is seven?" Lucas asked.

Jerry paused. "July?"

"Right. Okay, so the second number is the day of the month, and the third number is the year. I'll have to drive you guys back in the van and pick up the car later. Come on, you're late for school."

But the boys stood together, not moving. Tony cleared his throat

"We brought you something," he said. "For the funeral."

Sean lifted the trunk of the Oldsmobile. Inside the space was filled with cut hothouse flowers laid helter-skelter: spider mums, snapdragons, roses, gladioli, baby's breath. The car smelled like a florist's display.

Lucas shook his head. "I'm not going to ask you where you got this stuff because I don't want to know."

"You're right man," Jerry grinned. "You don't want to know."

"Shit man, all we did was *ask*." Sean fidgeted with his jacket.

"In a nice way."

"Sure, Kendo *always* asks in a nice way, don't he?"

Lucas said nothing.

"Hey, Mister Lucas," Tony began again. "Could we, like, put them near where you buried the wolf? I mean, to show respect? Is that okay with you?"

They followed Lucas up the trail silently, carrying the flowers through the morning woods. When they came to the stones and fresh earth, they knelt and laid the flowers down. The hothouse blossoms looked incongruously tropical in the dirt and dead leaves. Already the gladioli had wilted and browned in the sun.

They stood for a while, listening to the wind in the trees. A quail called, close by.

At last Tony cleared his throat, clenching his hands in his jeans pockets. "Um, wolf," he said slowly, his eyes focused on the trees beyond. "We came here today to show that we were sorry you died. Because we thought you were great. I mean, I know people said you were bad because you were a killer. And we just wanted you to know we didn't think that. And we came here because we are your brothers.

"So," Tony took a deep breath. "So goodbye."

Tony stepped back and made the sign of the cross, touching forehead, heart, and shoulders. Kevin and Sean followed. "In the name of the Father, and of the Son, and of the Holy Spirit, Amen," Jerry murmured, nodding his head at the holy names.

Kendo slapped his hands twice, placed his palms together with the fingers flat close to his face, and bowed stiffly from the waist, summoning the spirits.

As he turned to go, Tony felt the tears come again, but this time there was no pain with them. Lucas's hand touched his shoulder, and, for a moment, he laid his cheek against the rough cloth of Lucas's shirt.

In the stillness, the quail called again, *bobwhite, bobwhite*. Farther away, a pheasant racketed out of a sumac bush.

"We better go on back." Lucas ruffled Tony's hair. Single file, they picked their way down the stony path. Lucas glanced about, searching for something to teach, to break off the awkward moment.

"Hey, you know you can eat these?" Lucas knelt on a rock beside a clump of fiddleheads thrusting pale croziers through the oak leaves.

The kids crowded around him.

"They taste like asparagus. See, when they get bigger, they'll be ferns." Lucas gently peeled the fuzz off one tip and uncurled the tiny stem.

"No shit," Kevin said admiringly. "Can you eat all this stuff around here?"

"No, a lot of wild plants are toxic. Poisonous. When we get to Canada, I'll teach you what you can and can't eat so you can survive in the wild."

"Hey, how come you know all this stuff?" Jerry asked.

"Because I'm the Wolfman. Or was. I guess I'm not the Wolfman anymore." Lucas smiled.

"Hey man," Sean said. "You always be the Wolfman to us."

"You think we really goin' to Canada?" Sean asked.

"I think we can swing it. Right now, I got to get you guys to school."

In the warm sun, Lucas started the van and pulled out into the narrow road. He swerved sharply to avoid a box turtle.

"Stop the car!" Kendo said from the back seat. Lucas put on the brakes.

Kendo rarely spoke. When he did, it had an immediate effect.

Kendo slid out of the van and ran back to where the turtle sat on the yellow line, his feet and head drawn down inside the shell. Lucas switched on the van's flashers. "Hold him away from you," he shouted back. "They piss when you pick 'em up!"

Kendo held the turtle stiffly at arm's length, stepped over the ditch, and laid it gently in the tall grass. First, the head popped out, looked around with tiny black eyes, and then the scaly legs. The turtle heaved itself up, and marched toward the Big Blue.

Kendo got into the back seat and nodded gravely at Lucas. "He be all right now," he said.

"Hey, it's all right, man. We all right." Jerry grinned at Lucas. For a moment, Lucas studied their faces as a parent would look at a tiny child, seeing in them only hope.

"Hey Canada, watch out for the Wolfman of Beacon Hill," Kevin threw back his head and yowled. Sean poked him.

Lucas shook his head. Facing into the morning sunlight, he swung the van back, toward the city.